The Vampires Spell

Taken by The Night:

Book 1

Lucy Lyons

© 2017

Subscribe to our Newsletter!

This exclusive **VIP Mailing List** will keep you updated on our latest content. Subscribe and receive "The Vampire Kiss" absolutely FREE to your email and stay in touch with the latest updates to your email by clicking below.

GET ACCESS NOW

www.PersiaPublishing.com/subscribe-to-romance/

LIKE US AT

https://www.facebook.com/LucyLyonsRomance/

CAN YOU HELP?!

PLEASE leave a quick review for this book if it gives you any value. It provides valuable feedback that allows me to continuously improve my books and motivates me to keep writing.

Thank You!

© Copyright 2016 by Persia Publishing- All rights reserved.

Table of Contents

Chapter 1

I felt the first burning pain shoot through my legs as I crouched down and inhaled sharply before leaping from the rooftop to the one adjacent. With a quick roll I sprang back to my feet in a near seamless motion that propelled me back into a run. The sound of running footsteps was carried to my ears on the breeze, and two loud thuds, right on top of each other, sounded behind me. I increased my pace, ignored the burning in my chest, and gathered myself for another leap, this time to a pitched roof that I could slide down, forcing my pursuers to the ground.

Every muscle screamed at me as my target came into view. Running headlong through the gate of the large viaduct and into the stone tunnel, I skidded to a stop in front of an electronic panel disguised as a rusted out and moldy conduit. The door slid open and I threw back my shoulders and controlled my breathing. I strode purposefully toward a woman dressed in a sensible brown skirt suit, her hair pulled back into a severe bun at her neck. She glared balefully at me over horn-rimmed glasses and sighed as she jotted notes on her tablet with a stylus.

"Taking your new assignment a little seriously there, aren't you, Simi?" I snickered, finally leaning against the stone wall at the woman's back and puffing out my cheeks as I tried to fill my aching lungs with oxygen.

"What? I'm trying out a new look. I call it 'Van Helsing meets nurse Ratchet'." She did a little turn and then cleared her throat as the hunters that had been tailing me, Clayton and David, joined us in the alcove.

"It looks very professional and scary, but I for one will never forget that you are way scarier in black leather leggings than you are in a skirt," I informed her. She giggled and arched an eyebrow at the boys.

"Do you want to know your times?" She asked. Clayton groaned and shook his head. "Not if Caroline's been in here long enough to not even be breathing heavily." David shook his head too.

"I'm not especially interested, but if we tanked, I need to know where I screwed up," he confessed. "I straight lost her for a good thirty seconds. That's life or death, man." Simi smiled at David and batted her eyelashes, while Clayton and I rolled our eyes at each other and exchanged a fist bump on the low. It was no secret that Simi, and every other female he randomly encountered, was half in love with David. My apparent immunity to his dark brown eyes and long eyelashes was probably the reason we were still best friends. No one needed to know that I couldn't crush on him, because what I felt was so much deeper than his dark, brooding looks.

"Well, Caroline *did* shave five seconds off her time, which is a new best for her." I bowed at the neck and David laughed, putting his arm around me and squeezing me affectionately. I flushed and dropped my gaze, hoping he didn't notice my racing pulse, or at least credited my run for the breakneck thrumming in my veins.

"Awesome Care-Bear. You are already the fastest of us, now you're about to beat the standing record." I rolled my eyes at the childhood nickname I abhorred, but the compliment made my face warm with pleasure. A new best was worth the burning pain that was still fading in my lungs and thighs. Training with Clayton and David, two of the best overall students of the Venatores Lamiae, the society of vampire hunters, had pushed me to heights I hadn't imagined were possible when I first arrived.

"Clayton, your stats show that your jumps were some of your best, and you had a personal best by almost three feet in total footage. Well done. Now, if only you weren't panting like a vampire on the edge of sunrise, I'd tell you that you should be pleased with your performance."

"Well, if we're ever forced to chase a vampire with Caroline's speed and stamina for twenty miles on foot, there damn well better be a team on the other end to take over the heavy lifting," Clayton shot back as he pushed off the wall and headed towards the dormitory. "See you for lunch after I shower," he reminded me, pointing at me with both hands.

"You'll probably see me in the shower," I stammered as he wiggled his eyebrows, "I mean, in the bathroom. Ugh, you know what I mean, now go wash the stink off and stop grinning, you idiot." His cackle floated back to me as he disappeared around the corner of corridor that led to the student dormitories.

"Do you want to tell me something, Care-Bear?" David's face was a careful blank, but his eyes danced with amusement.

"Shut up." He scoffed at me and followed Clayton towards our rooms. Simi arched an eyebrow and handed me her tablet so I could review the route I'd taken and my vitals at each of the check points I'd passed.

"That was the longest training chase on record that I can see. Although, I'll have to look it up in the archives to be sure." Simi grinned at me. "You're such a badass. I can't wait until you swear in; I'm going to make you the scariest thing to come out of the Lamiae, like, ever." She placed one coffee-colored hand on my arm. "You did really well. I know you won't do it out here in front of the guys, but in your room? You've earned a victory dance." I chuckled and leaned into her.

"Once I can feel my legs again, I'll be sure to do that." I said goodbye and went to my dorm, keeping my pace steady and making sure I didn't favor my aching right knee, which was jarred and painful from my last drop. I'd mistimed the last step and almost blown the kneecap. Weakness wasn't permitted among the Lamiae, and us students were careful to show ourselves to be capable to face the demons we aimed to eradicate. I wanted to graduate top of my class just like David was about to. Those who scored the highest marks were given highest priority in assignments and the best hunters to train with. I had top marks in every subject, from History, to Chemistry, to Vampire Anatomy. I wasn't about to let a bad landing screw it up for me.

I stripped down to my bra and panties, and iced my knee while I pulled the course up on my laptop and reviewed my weakest moments. Aside from my last drop from roof to ground level, I had three other major slows, all in places where I had to make a choice. I opened a scheduling tab and reserved a few blocks of time in the reflexes chamber. Quick on my feet, but slow to decide. Sounded like me, all right.

I took the ice pack off my knee and threw it back in the freezer compartment of my first aid cabinet in the corner of my room. I took out my Xanax, and slipped a single pill into my pocket, out of habit more than necessity, since I hadn't had a panic attack I couldn't control in months. I wrapped my knee with an Ace bandage and put on sweats to wear to the shower, so the bandage wouldn't be visible.

David and Clay were done with their showers and were primping in front of the mirror when I arrived. Between them, they had as much hair and skin product as Simi, and she was a theatrical genius and a master of disguise.

"Hurry it up, slow-poke, or we'll have to eat without you, and you know, the cool kid table isn't cool when you're the only one sitting there." I flipped David off and walked away without answering. Chances were they'd still be doing their hair when I got out, and he knew it.

David was just packing up his hygiene kit when I stepped out, back in my sweats, with my wet hair soaking the back of my shirt. He tossed me his brush and I smoothed the wet tendrils into a respectable ponytail at my crown, stealing some of his moisturizer for my face and hands before we walked out together. A couple of younger students shot daggers at me as we passed them in the hall, but my skin was thick when it came to other women's hatred. It came with the territory, being raised alongside God's gift to women. Sure, he had chocolate eyes that looked right through you, a six-foot frame under the build of an all-American, and a perpetual tan, courtesy of his Brazilian heritage. Okay, so he was bloody beautiful, and sometimes, he was a little *too* aware of it.

But David wasn't just my best friend. He was my big brother. When I arrived at his house, I couldn't speak. I was so little, and the horror of watching my parents mutilated and killed for sport was more than I could process at the age of three. He was only one year older than me, but even then, he'd protected me and kept me safe. When I was old enough, David's parents, my new family, had explained the truth behind my memories and nightmares. That was when I learned vampires were real. It was also when my foster father showed me a photograph of a face I could never forget, no matter how hard I tried. This time though, the vampire's eyes weren't glowing red with hellfire like they were the night he visited my home: they were lifeless and clouded, his head lolling in a basket, severed from the rest of his body.

David had held my hand, trying to protect me from the image, but it didn't hurt to see the vampire's death. I'd felt such a fierce joy that it frightened me. My foster parents were hunters, members of the Venatores Lamiae, an elite cadre started by the Roman church millennia before to observe, hunt, and eradicate the scourge of vampirism. David had always been the one to stand between me and the world, and the more I stood on my own, the more he made me feel like I could do anything.

I sighed, the ache in my knee distracting and sharp. David didn't say anything. He just put his arm around me, draping my arm over his shoulders. It took the weight off my knee while making it look like besties just being affectionate. Because Clayton and I had done so well, our practice times had been broadcasted through the bunker and gossiped about, thoroughly. David and I walking like a couple of drunks in the middle of the day wouldn't even make them blink.

"So, did you hear a pop, or are you just sore?" He asked as we sat across the table from Clay.

"It twanged. Not a, full-on, pop." Clay gaped at us then muttered something under his breath as David got back up to get us lunch. "Clayton, what's up?" I asked.

"You ran the course injured, and you still kicked my ass."

"Well, it helps that I treat it like it's not practice. Every time. It's not you chasing me, it's him. Pretty damn good motivation, if you think about it."

"Okay, that's messed up. And probably exactly what I should be doing."

"I'm going to ask them to randomize the course again. Will you back me up?"

"But, we're just getting used to it. Oh, I get it. You're a slave driver, but yes I'll back you up. You really want to blow the records out of the water, don't you?"

"That's not what I was aiming for. I went over my run today, and every time I had to make a choice, I froze. I'm not like you and David. I don't even know anyone but you guys, Simi, and my teachers. I freeze. I have panic attacks. I'm afraid they'll stick me in a library and never give me a chance." David slid a tray in front of me, with a salad big enough for two people, and fragrant garlic bread.

"You haven't had a panic attack in a long time. You're unique here, and everybody agrees that you're special, Care-Bear," he said. I rolled my eyes at him.

"Girls who tell me I'm worthless sing my praises to you, David. They don't think I'm special. They want you to like them." Clay nodded, shrugging when David glared at him.

"Sorry bro. As your wingman, I can tell you she's on point. You two are scary together. I can't even imagine what it's going to be like with you guys running the place someday." He winked at me and I had to smile back. Clay's positivity was unusual around here, where every day was life or death, by necessity. "So, are we ready for some beach time?" David beat on the table like a drum and grinned.

"I'm already packed. How about you, squirt?" Clay chimed in.

"Yes, I'm packed. And if you call me squirt again, I'm going to break your legs." I drawled. I was as excited to get away as the guys, but nervous. It was the first time we were getting to go away without constant adult supervision, and I was anxious about losing my safety net and being around strangers at the same time. But Malibu sounded so amazing, and I couldn't wait to spend some time on the beach. Once David was apprenticed, he'd be up mostly at night. Clay and I had already decided that when he started night training, we would too, which meant a serious limit on time to bask in the sun.

I glanced at David out of the corner of my eye and thought about what Clay had said. I had no intention of coming in second to anyone in the Venatores Lamiae, but it made my chest feel tight, and my stomach heat up, to think of spending my near future even closer to David. I'd no longer be able to stand one step behind and watch him forget I existed when we weren't alone.

After we had finished eating, David snuck me into the nurses' station without our monitor, Simi, or any of the teachers seeing us, and cajoled the nurse into giving me a cortisone injection for my knee. She barely seemed to notice I was there, despite me being the patient, until I asked David to leave so I could talk to her about girl stuff. When he left, she gave me a death stare, until I pulled out some tears, just enough to make her feel guilty. I looked even younger than my seventeen years on my best day. My glassy eyes and red nose only knocked a couple more years off that. By the time I left, she'd handed over an additional injection "for an adult to give me if I needed it".

I also asked for more Xanax, and oral anti-inflammatories, which I'd add to my kit for emergencies.

Clay and David were both waiting outside the triage when I walked out. My pain had almost completely subsided already. David put an arm around me and I let him, even though I didn't need the support anymore. After all, who was I to turn down the support of my best friend?

Chapter 2

The entire class was buzzing with the conversations of twenty students as we all tried to guess what was keeping Eldritch. Our Anthropology professor was never late, and there were already speculations that he'd been called out on a hunt and wasn't coming back. But Eldritch was far too old to be actively hunting vampires, even if the thought of him being hospitalized did make most of us smile. I was set to be valedictorian of my class, top marks, never late or missing homework, and even I couldn't escape his foul temper. He swept into the classroom, and there was an audible groan from all of us at the sight of the black storm cloud in his expression. "Two more days 'til vacation", I thought. "Two more days".

"I have a special treat for you today, class." Eldritch spat out the words, literally, so that a fine mist settled on my desk and books. I forced myself to ignore it and not brush it away. I took comfort in the fact that it probably *was* going to be a treat for us. He seemed pretty unhappy, and he hated anything his students thought was fun. "I present to you," Eldritch continued, "Signora Borgia,

master of the eleventh order of magic and elder of the
Venatores Lamiae."

A collective gasp went up around the room as a
slender, pale woman glided to the front of the classroom
and bowed at her neck. This was the closest I'd ever been
to a true legend. Signora Borgia was a hunter and magic-
user. According to my textbooks, she'd been born to a
powerful Italian family of hunters, during the
Renaissance. She looked no more than twenty-five, which
meant she was an incredibly powerful sorceress. Magic
and psychic powers like her telepathy, incredibly rare,
meant that those with talents were the most valuable
members of the Venatores. Signora Borgia was the most
renowned of them all.

She looked at each of us in turn, and my throat went
dry as I waited for her to look at me. When her eyes finally
lit on my face, I felt an instant recognition, even before I
heard her voice in my head Startled by the invasive
sensation, I felt something like a door slamming shut
inside me. It was followed by the impression that
someone was pushing at it from the outside. My heart
raced and I shook, but my jaw locked and I couldn't speak

or tell her to stop. My foster parents had explained that my mind worked differently from others. Until now, I didn't understand what they'd been trying to say.

Her face registered surprise, and she stepped up to my desk, touching my forehead with one long, cool finger. She traced a series of symbols across the fevered skin above my eyebrows, starting at the right temple and moving across to end at the left.

"I am Dominique, Caroline. It is fascinating to meet someone so young who has raw, untrained psychic ability," she projected telepathically, her voice an echo inside my head that gave me goosebumps. "I regret frightening you. Please come out, I'm not here to harm you." Her being washed over me, entreating me to be calm, but I didn't know how to control what I was doing. I had built my psychic walls in a terrifying instant, unaware of what I was doing. When Venatores doctors had noticed this ability in me, they had called it traumatic disassociation. They said is wasn't a valid psychic ability, but a one-time herculean effort to save myself. I wasn't excited about proving them wrong in the middle of class.

The spot where Dominique had touched my forehead began to cool, in swirls and symbols that followed the spell, or whatever she had done to me. I felt my jaw unlock gradually and my walls melted away like ice. It wasn't at all like the violent tearing down that I would have expected. I took a deep breath and thanked her, using her telepathic connection. Dominique rewarded me with a smile that warmed me to my toes.

"Now that Caroline is finished interrupting class, let's carry on with the lesson, shall we?" Professor Eldritch's acerbic tone made Dominique's eyes fly wide, and then she winked at me.

"Oh, I agree, Professor. In fact, I'd like Caroline to join me at the front for a demonstration She's going to be my guinea pig, and help me teach a vital skill that every hunter should know." Eldritch motioned for me to join the sorceress at the front of the class; his jaw was working under his skin like he was grinding hard enough to break his own teeth.

"Now, can you explain to the class what happened when I touched your mind?" Dominique asked. I hesitated, unsure of how to explain without speaking of my parents, a secret that only David and his parents were privy to. I'd prefer the whole school think I was weird and shy and a nerd. I wasn't sure I could stand pity or fear from them.

"I. Um, I had a really bad experience as a child. The kind of thing that no one can really describe without making the room super uncomfortable, so, I won't go there. But, when it happened, I was little... barely talking in full sentences, little." I cleared my throat. "So, when I was found after the bad thing happened, I wasn't speaking. The doctors called it 'catatonic'," I shared, looking straight at Dominique, and pretending the class wasn't even there. "But my foster brother seemed to always know what I wanted, how I was feeling, and what I wanted to say, even though I was silent for a long time."

"You shared a psychic connection?" Dominique questioned.

"That's what my foster parents guessed, but we were never sure. I went to therapy and tore down the walls that I built to protect my mind, over a long time, one brick at a time." I swallowed hard. "I threw them back up the moment I felt you in my head. How did you get them down so easily?" The sheer power I'd felt pushing at me was terrifying. I questioned my right to be at a school with kids so brave and ready to fight monsters that I couldn't even imagine without giving myself nightmares.

"That, in fact, is exactly why I am here." Dominique smiled at me like I'd just discovered a new element of magic. "The first thing any student should learn, even before they learn to hunt, is how to protect their own minds from intrusion. Vampires are highly developed predators. They have the upper hand in almost every situation, and many can even infiltrate minds, like I did when I entered the room. I'm going to spend a few days with you, teaching you how to keep your minds safe." She motioned me to my chair, and I sank to the wooden seat with shaky legs.

Eldritch sat in the corner behind his desk, and I glanced at him when I felt his eyes on me. His face was unreadable as he watched me, but the scrutiny was enough to make my palms damp, and I fingered the pill in my pocket like a touchstone.

Signora Borgia explained the visual of mental blocks. She said we each had to have them ready at our command, without putting any thought into it. She also explained that when shields were automatic, but not cultivated and practiced, like mine, they were much easier to break down. To prevent this, she gave us instructions for building our strongest, best mental shields.

Class had gone almost an hour over before Eldritch finally released us. I was gathering my books and waiting for the crowd pressing out the door to thin so I could make my escape, when Dominique and Eldritch approached my desk.

Dominique addressed me. "Caroline, I would like to give you one extra bit of homework before you go. You are the only student in the class who can accomplish it, and I feel that it would be of use to you right away to have it." I nodded, and she handed me a notebook. "This is my first spell book. I was your age when I started to exhibit talents, and I was obsessed with writing down everything I learned, because I had no one to teach me." I looked at the ancient leather binding in awe. "It was a different time then, and I have no doubt you will surpass me in time, given some instruction and time to realize your strength." She opened the vellum pages to a section marked with a red silk ribbon. "This spell will help you bring anyone back to themselves. If another controls them or if they are hysterical with fear or even rage this spell, done correctly, will bring them back to their rational mind." I read the words silently, mouthing them as I did.

"I have used that spell to bring even vampires out of their blood fugue," Eldritch added. His face was grave, but the resentment and irritation that usually marked our conversations was absent. "You are too fragile to be here, Caroline. I have always thought that, and my opinion hasn't changed. However, with this, I think your chances of survival are greatly improved."

"Thank you, professor," I replied. "I hope that all my hard work helps too." For a moment, I could have sworn I saw compassion in his eyes. In a flash it was gone and his crusty demeanor was firmly in place.

"By hard work, I hope you mean you're going straight back to your room to practice," he drawled. He held the door open and gestured me through. I nodded my thanks to both him and the Signora, and escaped before he came up with anything more cutting to chase me out the door.

I jogged back to my dorm room, texting David on the way. He was thrilled that people were seeing my true abilities. All I felt was the crushing weight of more possible failures chasing me down as surely and physically as the undead we hunted.

He asked me to meet him outside, in the park that the society had built around the viaduct entrance. He also warned me to wear my sneakers. I pulled a scoop neck t-shirt over my head and added a light jacket that I tied around my waist. I'd learned after years of unplanned adventures with David that a twenty-minute walk could turn into hours of tailing random people for practice, or breaking into warehouses and running rooftops in the dark. Everything he did was to further his one goal: to carry on the family legacy as a Venatores Lamiae master-hunter. No one understood that better than I did, and he knew I was on his side, no matter how much trouble we got in after.

The air was cooler than I expected as I slipped out the back door through the viaduct, but this wasn't exactly a shock for the Pacific Northwest. Our teachers gave us a curfew because we knew something the public around us didn't, and our knowledge made us targets. David (and Clayton, who was with him) had scouted around the back door and made sure it was clear and no one, inside or outside, had seen us leaving.

"Hey, Care-bear, the clouds are thick tonight. There's no telling what he's going to want us to do," Clayton quipped. I nodded and hid my smile behind my hand as David rounded the corner. Even in the half light of the street lamp, I could see the flush that darkened his naturally olive skin. He held out a card to me, and I peered at it in the light.

"A fake ID?" I arched an eyebrow. "I'm not even going to ask how you got someone to make this."

"Good strategy. You should do that more often," he teased. "We're going on vacation, to a resort with poolside bar service. I, for one, want to give these a trial run before we try them out of state." I shrugged and slipped the fake driver's license in the clear plastic pocket of my wallet, then zipped my real one into the change purse so I wouldn't get confused and show the wrong one after a beer or two. After all, if I had two beers, that would take my lifetime grand total up to three. I wouldn't bet that I could win any drinking contests, and I didn't want to try.

The night seemed to take on a more ominous chill as I considered exactly how far south the night could go, but I kept my mouth shut. I wasn't brave, but I wasn't a snitch, and if I didn't go and someone noticed the boys' absence, I'd be the first person called to the Dean's office.

David stayed close to home, but far enough that we didn't run too much of a chance bumping into anyone we knew. My heart was in a vice as we stepped up to the door, knowing my stupid little girl face was going to give us away, and I hesitated at the steps. The bar was dingy and poorly lit even on the outside, just like the ones in the movies. A Bud Light sign in the window flickered and blinked from an electrical short, and when we walked in and showed our ID's, the bouncer barely spared us a glance. We could've used our real ID's and no one would've been the wiser. I filed the information away for later and let David lead us to a high-top table.

A pretty, blonde lady in a low-cut tank top and shorts that were far too short for comfort on wet, cold Seattle nights, appeared at my elbow, making me jump.

She wasn't there for me though, and soon, David had her swooning. I looked away, working to unclench my jaw and school my face into a more neutral expression than what I felt in the churning pit of my stomach. Perhaps his skill at mindless flirtation was a psychic talent, that he could make panties of any age drop, just by smiling. I watched the other patrons of the bar as the waitress took our orders and promised to be back soon. I even managed not to growl at her when she touched David on the arm before strutting away.

"Damn man, normally I love being your wingman, you know that. But now, it's just getting depressing," Clay complained. I giggled and shot Clay a wry smile. We both knew the truth, that he'd have given anything to be David, and I'd have given anything to be with him. He was right. It was depressing.

"So, Dominique Borgia hijacked my anthropology class today," I blurted, eager to change the subject.

"No kidding. She doesn't come around every year; you must have some talent in your class," David mentioned, slamming his mouth shut as the waitress appeared right at his side with pints of dark amber beer for each of us. I didn't answer, and Clay made an exasperated sound.

"Seriously, why am I friends with either of you. You're giving me an inferiority complex!" He half-laughed as he spoke, but I saw the shadow that passed over his eyes.

"You're friends with us, because you're the fastest, strongest guy in your graduating class, and anyone with a quarter of a brain wants you at their back when stuff goes down," I reminded him. "I broke my own record today, and you almost caught me, with a lead." I glanced at David, encouraging him to help me make Clayton feel better, but he rolled his eyes, his mouth set in a frown.

"Well, that's true," Clay mused. "If you hadn't done the last three miles on a busted knee, I'd feel pretty good about myself." Now it was Clay who rolled his eyes, but this time I giggled.

"Help me out here, David?" I asked. David didn't say anything, and I peered over at him. His face had gone dark and angry. I knew he couldn't stand that anyone, even Clayton, had performed better than him. I touched his hand and smiled. "You two are the best in your class. I wish I was graduating with you, and I didn't have to wait another year," I confessed. It was enough to salve his ego. The storm clouds cleared and he smiled at me.

"Sorry, Caroline. wish you were coming with us too."

"I love you guys. I'll miss you after graduation," I replied. My heart beat like it could burst out of my chest, and I mentally cheered as I managed to keep my face calm. David seemed happier, but something had changed in the air, and after only one beer, the guys were as ready to sneak back into the compound as I was. David paid the bill, snickering to us as he showed us the name and phone number written on the back of his receipt. Clay sputtered and threw up his hands in mock dismay.

"Marry young, David, or I'll never have a chance at a girl." David was in better spirits as we split up to sneak in at our favorite spots, and I sighed and kicked a loose rock outside the vent I used to sneak back into my wing of the dormitory. Boys might be the death of me, I thought. But, I had Dominique's present waiting for me.

With a satisfied smile, I dropped down into my room from the vent above my bed and picked up the little leather booklet Dominique had given me. The spell was simple enough, even though it was in Latin, for which I was grateful. My grasp of dead languages wasn't as good as the ones I could Google translate if I got stuck.

I read the words three or four times, then sat at my desk with a small mirror in front of me and practiced my shields. With the three of us going away for Spring break, it couldn't hurt to have some practice and extra protection. I stared into the mirror, then closed my eyes and visualized my new psychic shields.

Dominique had explained that mine was brittle, and more likely to shatter than it should have been, even though I'd had it so long. So, instead of brick, like the house I'd lived in before a vampire drained my parents before my eyes, I visualized smooth forged steel. Impenetrable and cold, it began far under the earth in my mind's eye. I let it flow up out of the earth as though it grew naturally, so it was as much a part of nature as if it had been a tree or mountain. I pushed until I felt faint, stretching the wall up and over me until I could see it closed around me, like a tower or a bullet casing.

I opened my eyes and in doing so caught my reflection in the mirror. I was sweating, beads gathering on my upper lip and rivulets of the salty stuff dripping down the sides of my face. I sent up a prayer to whoever might be listening that my life wouldn't depend on this skill anytime soon, and turned off my desk lamp. I had one more day of classes before break and the vacation of a lifetime. Knowing David, I figured that meant I needed to sleep while I could.

Chapter 3

David held my hand as the plane took off and I tried to control my nervous twitching. I wasn't sure if it was my first plane trip or his fingers intertwined with mine that was making me so nervous. Clay was across the aisle, and I sat between them, thinking I was less likely to panic if I wasn't in a window seat. In my pocket was my emergency medicine cabinet, but I clung to David and focused on the pressure of his hand, while Clay distracted me from the shaking and bouncing with his easy conversation.

Even with their support, and a few trips to the lavatory to splash cold water on my face and practice my shielding, I was still a wobbly mess when we deplaned, and had to fight the urge to kiss the dirty concrete when my feet hit the ground. I felt for the pill in my pocket, grateful that I'd managed not to use it. It had been so long since I'd had to take anything for my anxiety and I was starting to think I might finally have the tools not to need them anymore.

We passed a trash bin on the way to the luggage carousels, and I dropped the pill in. A wave of panic swept over me, but passed, and when I caught up to the guys and our luggage, I was still smiling. Clayton got the keys to the rental car and before I knew it we were heading down a palm tree lined drive. We came to a large iron gate that closed in the exclusive resort we'd saved, begged, and borrowed to be able to afford.

David showed the guard our reservations and he opened the gates. The excitement in the Jeep was palpable. It only increased when the first hit of salty ocean air filled my lungs, and I was sure the bikinis that the guys found themselves surrounded by didn't hurt their mood at all. We had a suite; the guys in one room on two queens, me in the lock off on a king. I teased them about the advantages of being the only girl, and they came back with a refusal to let me lock the door.

I laughed, but secretly I was happy it meant that neither of them would be bringing anyone back to their room. I was okay with that. David was the first in his swimsuit and he ordered me downstairs as soon as I had put my things away. Clayton paused in my doorway on his way out, his ultra-pale Irish skin making me smile.

"Hey, good job on that plane ride, miss anxiety," he teased. "Proud of you." I blushed as my grin split my face.

I had ridden on an airplane, and done it without any medicine. I was in a new state, in a strange room, without an adult in sight to run to if things went south. My heart pounded and my hands shook as I pulled out the swimsuit I'd let Simi talk me into. It was the tiniest thing I'd ever seen, the hot pink fabric shaping to my chest in triangles so small I looked like I *had* a chest.

The bottoms weren't much better so I wrapped my sarong around my hips and paced my room for ten minutes before working up the courage to go down to the pool with the guys. I put on the large brimmed hat I'd bought on impulse and left the room. Down the wide marble stairs at the salt water infinity pool I knew I'd find the guys, flirting with girls who thought they had money.

I saw them before they saw me, but David's eyes followed me as I rounded the pool and sat down next to them. The look of sheer shock that flitted across his face thrilled me, but the one that followed made me grateful I was already sitting. His brown eyes went almost black as they filled with something I'd never seen from any man before. It was dark and possessive and so utterly masculine that my throat closed off and my face and neck crimsoned.

"Woah, Caroline," Clayton blurted. "Like, damn, girl!" He gave a low whistle and I laughed and shook my head.

"I can always count on you to make me feel less nervous, Clay," I laughed. "Thank God you're here. I'd probably be depressed otherwise, when I got home and no one noticed me." He arched his eyebrows at me.

"Fat chance, honey. Don't worry, we won't let anybody carry you off to be their sex slave." I gasped and stammered.

"I'm going for a swim. You guys are really something else." I poked Clayton in the ribs as I passed him, then handed him my hat as an afterthought. "You better have put on sunscreen, or the hunters are going to think we brought home our very own sun-roasted vampire by the time we leave." David chuckled and tossed Clay the sun block that had been laying on the table between the chaise lounges. Clay complained that he had no one to apply it, but just as I held out my hand for the tube of lotion, David stepped between us.

I couldn't see David's face, but Clay's went pale, then sunburn red, in an instant. His jaw clenched and his hands fisted at his sides, but like a flash, it was over, and I was left wondering if I'd imagined it. I would've written off his sudden change of mood if the guys hadn't been clashing more frequently than I'd noticed before. I took David by the hand and pulled him to the side of the pool.

"Whatever is going on between you guys, you need to get it figured out, David," I cautioned him. "Clayton and I are your friends. Don't push us away."

"Clayton and I, huh? It used to be you and me then him, remember?"

"Not likely I'd forget, David. But, I made room for him, even though it made me jealous sometimes." He scoffed. "No, really," I continued, "You guys can talk about stuff and have things in common that make me feel left out. Whatever you think he's done, or said, let it go. He's your friend. He'd kill for you, dumbass."

David rubbed his hand across the back of his neck. He nodded and waved to get Clay's attention. I should've known that he was up to no good, because he agreed so quickly. But, it was still a complete shock when the ground disappeared from under my feet. I hit the water with a shriek and surfaced to the sight of both guys clutching their sides, laughing. I sank to the bottom and launched myself straight up like I was roof running, and grabbed David's shoulder and Clay's shorts. Their faces changed from mocking to shock as I pulled them into the water on top of me, submerging us all.

When we had recovered, we hung on the edge of the pool near the snack bar. It wasn't long before we found another girl to make us a foursome and played chicken in the middle of the pool. I sat on David's shoulders, and the redhead on Clay's. Despite being in the water, it wasn't long before I was completely parched, and asked David if he'd come with me to get drinks.

"Clay actually offered to buy this round," David replied.

"True story, Caroline, let me grab my wallet." Clay came back with his wallet and my hat and we walked to the bar. I listened while Clay pointed out the tropical flora that the resort had put in, which didn't belong in the area. He was well-versed in herbology, but I'd never thought of how that information could matter, outside of the all-important salves that hunters used to prevent vampires from using glamor and clouding their minds. I was impressed and told him so, and laughed as he blushed.

"It's just me, Clay, I can admit to you that you're good at stuff," I teased. He smiled, but didn't say anything in response. He bought fruity drinks for me and the redhead, Tracy, and beers for himself and David. It seemed that whatever had gone on between the guys had passed, and I tried to let go of the sensation that there was another shoe about to drop.

Tracy was with her older siblings and their families. She was happy to tag along with us to avoid becoming the nanny to her nieces and nephews. I was grateful for one more reason to avoid mentioning hunter-things and to just relax. Clayton was like a puppy, serving her hand and foot and buying her lunch, plus all her drinks. She kept watching David, but I chalked it up to his unidentified talent and ignored it. After all, he was almost as generous with me as Clay was with his new friend.

We agreed to meet up with Tracy for a late supper and dancing at the club on the resort. We went to our rooms to relax, check in with our respective responsible parental-types, and wash off the salt. The sun was already low in the sky when we walked down to the garden to meet Tracy. I felt a chill down my spine that had nothing to do with the temperature, and everything to do with the recognition that when that golden orb disappeared, the monsters would come out to play. I'd been at the Venatores school for so long, I couldn't remember the last time I'd stopped to enjoy a sunset, instead of fearing them.

I'd felt confident in my little black dress, until we met up with Tracy and another girl she'd brought with her. Both were dressed to the nines, more skin showing than covered. I felt frumpy in my short black strappy dress and sandals. Tracy still had eyes for David, and I suppressed my usual twinge of jealousy and irritation when she brushed up against him and batted her eyelashes. I was sure David would never hurt Clay by encouraging her, and she would be gone in a day or two anyway.

The restaurant was busy, so we were encouraged to sit at the bar while we waited. We filed into the narrow bar area, with me on one side of David, and Tracy on the other, and Clay sandwiched between the two girls. On another day, I would've made a joke about how lucky they were. But, her persistent attention toward David and her inattention to Clay were getting under my skin.

When I saw her hand on David's thigh, my kettle reached the boiling point. I felt hot rage rise in me like steam, ready to pour out my mouth if I didn't keep it closed. I grabbed David's arm and forced him to turn towards me, making her hand fall away.

"What the hell are you doing, David?" I hissed at him, trying to keep my voice low enough to avoid a scene. "You *know* Clay likes her. You *know* that you can have any girl you want. Why can't you just once, just one damn time, tell someone 'no', and have a little integrity?"

"Seriously? You're going to do this here?" He jerked his arm out of my grasp.

"I'm not doing anything. I'm asking you not to do this to your friend." I looked at him, but hardly recognized the petulant, selfish boy in front of me.

"Okay, you want me to say 'no'. I get it," he paused and glanced over his shoulder at Tracy, then faced me and looked me in the eyes. "No, Caroline. You need to let me go and understand that you and I aren't here for a romantic getaway. Go find yourself a nice guy, no one is stopping you." I felt cold. The color drained from my face and I felt lightheaded. I imagined knocking him from his barstool with a stiff right to his jaw, but instead, took a deep breath.

"I hope she's worth it, David," I murmured, leaning in so he could hear me. "I can't help but wonder what you're going to do when you get home, without the friends you left with. Are you sure that her attention, her liking you, is really worth losing the two people who always have your back?" I slid off the barstool and stormed away without waiting for a response. I was too angry and hurt to pay attention to the niggling fear that still sat between my shoulder blades.

Unfortunately, as every hunter worth their salt knows, anger is a great way to lose focus. It's the one emotion that causes more stupid choices and deaths to our kind than any other outside factor. But I wasn't a hunter yet. I rushed headlong through the garden of tropical flowers, trying to find the shortest path to my room.

I strayed from the path and almost instantly stepped on a loose stone that kicked my already injured knee out at a bad angle. I cried out in pain and fell hard, sitting in the dirt, in the dark. I cursed David and my knee and the stupid idea to take a vacation in the first place.

"What a great first day of vacation," I said aloud to myself.

"Are you talking to me?" replied a thickly accented voice far too close behind me. I whipped my head around, but could only see the silhouettes of flowers and palm trees on a canvas of shadows. My pulse sped up and I swallowed past a lump in my throat. "No, sorry, I was talking to myself. I tripped. Have a good night!" I called out lamely. The darkness shifted when I looked back over my shoulder. My stomach clenched and heaved. Something was there that didn't want to be seen.

"You shouldn't be out here in the dark alone. Let me walk you to your hotel." The voice was closer, but no matter where I looked, no one was there. Fear crept up my spine as psychic power poured over me. This wasn't like

Lady Borgia's power, that I felt inside my head. The power I felt now made me blind to whatever it was I felt breathing on my face.

"I am a student of the Venatores Lamiae. You will hear from them, if you touch me," I gasped.

"Venatores," the voice in the darkness scoffed. "What use do they have for pretty, tiny creatures like you?"

There was a whoosh of air and a disembodied hand grabbed my throat, squeezing tightly enough that I could choke out raspy whispers, but not scream for help. An earthy smell of sweat and mold and decay filled my nose and I struggled harder, to no avail.

The monster held my throat and pinned me to his chest, his clawed hand over my heart, as though we were lovers. I trembled and he sighed, his foul breath moving my hair. In my last conscious moment I felt his papery, dry lips on my temple. Sheer terror swept through my mind as I threw up my psychic shields, my last defense against the evil that overcame me.

Chapter 4

My head was on fire. I was so disoriented that it took a moment to realize that I hurt almost everywhere else, too. My knee screamed with sharp, stabbing pain when I shifted, and it was hot and swollen to the touch. Even though I wasn't bound, the darkness of my surroundings was so thick that I had the sensation of being all alone in a vast emptiness. My heart pounded harder and I put my hand in my pocket for the little oblong pill automatically, before I remembered it was gone.

I began to hyperventilate, bright stars appearing in my vision against the pure black canvas all around me. I struggled to my knees and put my forehead on the cool stone floor to focus and calm down. I slowly erected my mental shields, picturing them shutting out the darkness and the stars, until I no longer felt blind. I reached out the way Signora Borgia had begun teaching us, visualizing my mind like fingers stretching out in front and around me. As I reached out with my mind I could feel, almost see, the wall ahead of me. Emboldened by my success I crawled forward, dragging my hurt leg behind me, until my fingers met cool, dry stone. This stone was cut in blocks. I traced a line of mortar laterally until I found a corner and continued along that wall until I brushed a doorframe with my fingertips.

I used the frame to inch myself into a standing position, grateful that the ceiling was high enough above my head that I couldn't touch it. Exhaling the breath I'd been unconsciously holding in a heavy sigh of relief, I ran my hands over the door. The door was made of a thick steel frame with wooden slats. I felt air move against my face, and as I slid my hands up the center of the door to the slight breeze, I found a barred window trimmed in the same cold steel as the door itself. I decided if there was a door, and a window, then at least I wasn't in a stone box. I'd found my exit. I sank to the floor in relief as my legs, which were like useless wet noodles, collapsed under me.

I was in trouble, obviously. But, I wasn't sealed in a crypt. A crypt wouldn't have doors with windows, just stone boxes for dead, or undead, bodies. It seemed a ridiculous thing to want, but I half-hoped I'd been stolen by organ thieves. I was barely a student of the Venatores lamiae, but I still knew how to fight a human and win, even injured.

Even I as I dared to let that hope form in my head, logic, and the sheer blackness around me, shot me down. I breathed in deeply and reached out with my other senses, trying to get any clue of where I was despite my blindness. The walls around me were dry, but the air that whispered over my face was musty and damp.

It was impossible to tell the time of day and after finding the corner farthest from the door, I put my back into it and listened for anything approaching through the corridor outside my cell. It was only going to be a matter of time before whomever, whatever, had taken me was going to come back. I had no intention of being caught off-guard again.

In my cell, the darkness and silence felt like an endless night. I couldn't imagine what perverse creature could find comfort in a life underground. If my captors returned and tried to turn me, I swore to myself that I would force them to kill me.

"Kill or be killed, I guess," I said to myself, jumping at how loud my voice sounded in the darkness.

"Oh my God, hello?" A young, female voice floated back to me in the darkness. I jumped again, my heart racing. Why hadn't I considered I wasn't alone?

"Hello!" I called out. "Who's out there?"

"I'm Becca. I'm in a dark room, it's so black in here." She sounded distant, like she was at the other end of whatever hallway joined our cells.

"Yes, there's a window in the door of the cell. But it's so dark. The entire corridor must be sealed off from light." Silence enshrouded me again, and in a panic, I called out to her, just to hear her voice. "Becca, can you guess how long you've been here? Or tell me how you were taken?"

"I was staying at the Fairfield resort in Malibu. I went to a beach party with my friend. A man grabbed her, I screamed, and that's the last thing I remember before waking up here."

"Okay, can you move around? Try measuring your room with steps. Find the door."

"Yes. Okay."

I stopped talking for a few seconds, trying to stay calm in the heavy silence so she could concentrate. I counted out thirty seconds in my head, then forty, before she screamed.

"Becca! Becca, tell me what happened!"

"Kenzie? Kenzie?" I heard her repeat a name. It sounded like she was crying, but not immediate danger.

"Becca!" I called out again, "What happened. What's going on?"

"Kenzie isn't answering."

"Are you sure it's your friend?" I thought fast. If they were putting more than one girl in a cell, maybe we were due for more company.

"Yes, she had her hair in a braid."
"Okay, good. Touch her face. Can you feel her breathing?" I waited.

"Yes, yes, she's alive!" Becca sobbed, her voice thick with emotion. "Oh, God, Kenzie, wake up!"

"Becca, how long have you been awake?"

"Only since right before I heard you." I thought for a moment. I must have been taken long before the others, and whatever they'd done to put me out had worn off, but not before they'd come back with Becca and her friend.

"Becca, I'm sure she'll wake up soon, okay, just stay calm, and we'll figure this out together," I reassured her, trying to ignore the sick feeling in the pit of my own stomach. I'd been awake for at least a couple of hours, but who knew how long the effects would last.

In a panic, I ran my fingers down the line of my neck on both sides, following the carotid artery and jugular veins. I did the same with my arms, checking the veins at my elbows and wrists. I was almost afraid to continue, but I undid my pants and slid them off. I felt over my hips, down my thighs, and down my legs to my ankles. No bite marks. I hadn't been bitten anywhere on my body.

I started shivering; if it was with relief, or from shock, I had no idea. Tears formed a lump in my throat and I hugged my knees to my chest and rocked while I cried until I could speak again. Becca and I had been silent for a few minutes, as she tended to her friend, but I had to know if either of them had been bitten either.

"Hey, Becca, are you still there?"

"Yeah, are you all right?" She paused before continuing. "It's okay if you're crying. I was too. I just meant are you hurt?"

"I'm fine. I do need you to do something for me. I need you to check your veins for puncture marks." I sighed, waiting for the questions that would lead to her telling me I was crazy.

"Do you think the guys that took us injected us with drugs?" It was as good a reason as I could give without sounding like a lunatic, and she was already in a black hole with no idea if her friend was hurt or sick. I was worried a vampire had put her under so deeply that she might never wake up.

"Yeah," I replied, rubbing my face with my hands. "So, you know, anything like that. It might not even be noticeable, except for a sore spot over a vein, like... like a bruise you don't remember getting." I took a shaky breath. "I checked myself, and I didn't find anything, I just want us all to be sure. Your friend,"

"Mackenzie."

"Right, Mackenzie. When she wakes up, we'll have her do the same thing to herself."

"I'm doing it now." Stuck in the dark halfway from nowhere I couldn't see or hear her moving, so I had to take her word for it. Maybe all the time in the dark or the time in the Venatores lamiae had made me paranoid. "The only bruise I have is on my butt. Maybe that's where they stuck the needle. It's pretty sore." I grinned. With no easy access to major arteries or veins, it was unlikely she'd been bitten on her butt. Her voice was as giddy as I felt.

We were stuck in the dark, hungry, and I was about to have to pee in a corner. But, we were alive, and fang-free, at least for the moment. I felt fresh tears sting my eyelids, but I was okay. Becca was okay and hopefully Mackenzie would be okay. The next step was to figure out how to get free, or get word to David and Clay, so the hunters could come for us.

There was so much I didn't know yet, so many things that weren't taught to us until we'd been initiated. So I started with what I did know: the truth and the lore of vampires.

Chapter 5

Becca and I chatted for a long time about where we came from, who we were, and how we got taken. We talked so long that I started to worry about her friend, Mackenzie. The upside was that we'd been gone long enough for David and Clayton to notice, and that meant hunters were already looking for us. I hated that my own stupidity and jealousy had left me alone and off-guard. I'd practically begged to be taken by naively wandering off on my own. David and Clayton had probably been happy to be rid of me, the fifth wheel of the group.

Before dating had become a focus of their lives, we'd been inseparable. I should have known it was inevitable that I'd be the one who didn't fit in the group anymore. It was gut wrenching how easily David had chosen flirting with someone new over our lifelong friendship. I wondered if he'd ever thought we were family, or if that was just forced on him too.

I mentally slapped myself out of my self-pity and started thinking about the monsters instead. They could have killed us or infected us on the spot. That was unless we were being given to a master, as a gift or maybe food, if the master was old enough that he couldn't pretend to be human anymore. I shuddered, and bile rose in my mouth.

The ancient ones, the oldest of the vampires, had thin, papery skin stretched over their skulls and their teeth were so prominent that they appeared lipless. Their eyes burned like coal in braziers and their hair receded to mere tufts at their temples or ears. The illustrations in our textbooks, of the few ancient ones the hunters had been able to capture, were horrific and nightmare inducing. The textbooks said that masters that old were almost impossible to catch or kill, especially since they retreated from humanity.

But if the master still needed to eat, where were they getting their food? The thought made me nauseated, and I leaned my forehead against the wall to cool off and change my thought process. Hunters and vampires killed each other, but we tried to keep it civilized. We knew the consequences of war for the human world.

If the vampires that took us (if they *were* vampires and not kidney thieves after all) could fly, they had access to hundreds of years of wealth and the toys that came with them. I had done some research on the geography of the

California coast. Most likely we'd been taken because we were convenient. The pitting I felt in the stone of the walls could be from proximity to the ocean, where salt spray and ocean storms would have broken the stone down faster than in drier locations.

"Becca, Becca, how is Mackenzie doing?" I called out, becoming more alarmed that she still wasn't awake.

"Her breathing is shallow and uneven. I can touch her face. I even pinched her arm! She didn't wake up or even make a sound." That one statement turned my blood to ice in my veins. If they hadn't bitten us to put us under, then we'd been "glamoured" or charmed to knock us out, which meant that the vampires that took us had gotten inside our heads.

My shields hadn't been enough to protect me. I wasn't surprised, but I was still ashamed of my weakness. Perhaps Dominique had been wrong about my 'raw talent,' as she'd called it. Maybe I was in a cell about to be drained of my blood by an impossibly terrifying predator; maybe that was just my fate. The vampire that killed my mother and father hadn't bothered to kill me. Now, my destiny to die as fang-feed had caught up to me.

For a moment, I'd imagined myself as "the girl who lived". Now, I just felt stupid. My lip slid between my teeth to stop me from biting my fingernails, which would be the next thing in my mouth if I couldn't come up with some sort of solution. I might not have been much of an expert, but I was the closest thing Becca and the still-unconscious Mackenzie had to a hunter.

"Becca, slap her. Hard," I ordered. "Hit her as hard as you dare with your open hand. We're running out of time, and we need her awake."

"I'm not going to hurt her."

"Really? What chance do we have to get her out of here, if she's still unconscious?"

"You think beating her up will help us get her out?"

"I think getting her awake gives us a chance to fight together, or at least negotiate for our lives. Right now, she is dead weight we can't carry and she can't argue for her freedom if she's unconscious." I didn't think vampires had a parlay system, but I was willing to bet if we were all awake, we'd stay together, whereas if Mackenzie was still asleep, they'd take her first, because she'd be easier for them to feed on.

Distantly, I heard the familiar slap of an open palm against skin, and another, and a third. Becca was screaming at Mackenzie and slapping her again, and again; almost hysterical as she begged her friend to wake.

"Becca, stop!" I shouted down the hall. I repeated myself, and the only sound I heard was her sobbing. "I'm sorry Becca. You tried." There was a long silence, and I wondered if I'd lost my only friend in the darkness.

"Caroline?" Becca's hoarse voice sounded like she'd been crying for days.

"I'm here, Becca."

"She isn't awake, but she moved. Oh, my God, she moved!" I didn't have the heart to tell her what I feared. That the vampire that had put her under was awake, which meant it was night, or nearly so. My heart sank. We'd been here at least a full day, then, with no hunters showing up to save us. Worse, if the vampires had been sleeping, it wouldn't be long now before we had company.

I'd considered why we were still alive and unmarked, but I hadn't figured out what came next.

I felt my way back to the side wall using the torch, felt around until I felt the clip that locked it in place and lifted it out of the holder. I sat in a crouch, with my back against the far wall and butt resting on my heels. That way I could spring up and launch the torch at the face of the first blood sucker through the door.

I knew that I couldn't fight, but maybe I could make them mad enough to kill me fast. I no longer remembered the details of my parents' deaths; my mind hadn't wanted to hold most of the images even when I was young. Time had been my sweetest friend and stolen the remaining images from me over the years. However, I would never lose the terror and soul-numbing hate that filled me at the thought of seeing another vampire.   I tried to focus on the things Signora Borgia and Professor Eldritch had been teaching my Anthropology and Mythology of Vampires class. *Their energy came from living blood, but only the very strongest could stay awake during daylight hours. Their psychic powers were varied, just like humans. There were some who had no mental powers to*

draw upon, just like some couldn't fly, and others had
every imaginable power.

Obviously, we were dealing with one, or several maybe, that could get in our heads and glamour us. Poor Mackenzie was weak-willed enough, or had a master vampire strong enough, to completely roll her. In the books, people like her were called Renfields, after Bram Stoker's "Dracula". These were humans who could no longer think for themselves, sleeping when their master slept and doing their bidding without question.

If we'd been brought here at the same time, then maybe I was strong enough to fight it off, at least a little. I'd been awake for a long time, and it made sense that we'd been sitting down here all day. My stomach would attest to that, if nothing else. Becca had woken hours after me, but she had woken on her own. I was about to call out to her and check in on Mackenzie, when I heard a scream from that end of the corridor.

"Becca! Becca answer me!" I screamed into the darkness, pressing my face against the bars desperately wishing I could conjure a light in the darkness. Then, as though I'd created it with my mind, a tiny flare of light floated and bobbed in the far distance. As tiny as it was, it was blinding after the hours of darkness and my eyes burned behind my eyelids as I blinked and squeezed them shut tight, trying to acclimate to the change.

"Caroline!" Becca screamed, her voice breaking off into a choking sound, as the light flickered in place where I imagined her door would be.

"Becca!" She didn't answer, and I gripped the ancient, iron torch tighter, and fell back from the door, to the side opposite the hinges. The silence was thick enough to touch and my palms grew wet and slick against the metal as I waited to befall the same fate as Becca and her friend.

The seconds ticked on, and my thighs and arms began to cramp from the position I was holding. I strained to stay still and not give away my position, as I realized the light outside my door was growing brighter. I rolled my shoulders and shifted my weight from the balls of one foot to the other, ready to spring. My scant training might be enough despite aching muscles and lack of food to draw blood when I swung.

Chapter 6

There was a scraping sound of metal against metal as a key turned in the door. Then it swung open. In the light was the shadowed face of a beautiful girl, not much older than myself. But, the age that I sensed in my mind was much, much older than she appeared.

"Well, now!" she exclaimed in a sugary voice. "I bet Vittorio didn't catch *that* little ability of yours when he grabbed you." The lit torch moved directly in front of my face, blinding me, and I swung out blindly. "Now, now, little witch. No need for that," the girl chided in her lilting voice, as she grabbed the iron out of my hand like it was nothing. I heard the clatter as it hit the far wall and clenched my jaw to keep from whimpering. "Now, let's go get you cleaned up and fed, then you can tell me what other powers you've got, little witch. I'm always interested in a pretty girl who can feel me inside her." Despite the youthful sweetness of her voice, I trembled at the threat behind the sexual innuendo.

"Kill me now. I won't be made into vampire fodder," I hissed, my voice shaking.

"Oh, you're a tiny hunter." My eyes had gotten used to the soft torchlight and I could see her shake her head. "What kind of people are they, sending a tender little thing like you out all by herself? You poor thing. I'll take care of you."

"You'll protect me?" I asked my voice soaked in disbelief.

"Of course. Don't believe all you hear from one hateful, frightened group of racists, darling. I for one love sweet little morsels like you. I couldn't bear to let anyone else touch you, except the master." She held out her hand. I was walking hand in hand with her up a long spiraling set of stairs, when I realized she'd glamoured me again. I wrenched my hand away and she laughed in delight, a clear, lovely sound that froze me at my core, paralyzing me with terror.

Her hard, blue eyes held mine and I focused on my psychic shield, straining against her power pressing in on me until she pulled back, a look of genuine surprise on her face. She was silent after my small victory over her. My heart swelled with fierce pride and made me braver as I walked into the unknown behind her.

She left the torch in a sconce on the wall at the top of the stairs and pushed open a wooden door, like the one that had shut me into my cell, but far larger and heavier. She motioned me through with a bow at the neck and followed close enough behind me that her skirt brushed my legs. Occasionally I caught images from her that chilled me and each time she got me to react she would laugh at me. But, she couldn't really violate me, which made me glad, and seemed to frustrate her.

"You'd be surprised how enjoyable my company can be, little witch," she huffed, when I balked at a particularly explicit image she was projecting of the two of us.

"You know you and I are almost the same size and height, don't you?" I replied, refusing to acknowledge what I was starting to believe was her flirting.

"But you have so much more to learn and so much growing to do in here," she giggled, tugging my head back with one hand and tapping my temple. I fell silent again, hoping she would grow bored and leave me alone again. While we walked I concentrated on my shield until I wasn't sure if I had finally got it right, or she really had gotten bored and given up. I let the shield drop, and staggered as a picture of her bathed in my blood slammed me against the wall, choking on my own scream.

"Oh, Colette, leave her be. She isn't for you she is for the Master of the City." She turned to me "Child, you may call me Rachel." The voice was kinder and older, and hushed me as new power clamped down on my vocal cords. How could I hope to escape, or fight, when these beings had all the power they needed to make me submit to them against my will?

Colette, the vampire who had brought me up from the dungeon, huffed and stormed off to the far end of the room. She started brushing her hair, all the while watching me in the mirror. The older vampiress led me to a large copper bath in the middle of the room. It was big enough to hold four of me and was deep and steaming from the hot water under the fragrant bubbles. She took my hand and helped me into the bath, the water and lavender fragrance instantly beginning to unknot my aching muscles.

I watched Rachel as she took away my dirty dress and laid out fresh clothes, presumably for me. The care they were taking with my appearance was confusing.

Surely the master vampire I was meant to feed didn't require his food in the Victorian dress that was laid out in front of me? The grey-haired vampire saw me watching her and smiled gently.

"You are quite safe in here, no matter what Colette said to frighten you," she sighed. She picked up a thick sea sponge from a cart next to the bath and set it on the water in my lap. "Wash up, the master awakes, and he will have need of you."

"The Venatores will come for me," I said it softly, but she stiffened and turned back to face me.

"You are no hunter." She glanced at Colette over my head and I heard her tinkling laughter like shards of glass in my head. "Colette. Mind yourself. If she's broken when he gets her, he'll take it out on you." She looked into my eyes. "No. You are no hunter. Are you a ward of the society, then?" My face heated and she nodded. "They may very well come for you, but you are not the first ward of the hunters to disappear. They simply make more to replace those they lose, don't they?"

I ground my teeth together to stop anything worse from escaping my lips. Colette appeared within my view and scooped the sponge up from the water before I could protest. She watched my face while she gently washed me and I stayed frozen, knowing that if I let her see my fear she'd only make it worse. The sponge and her fingers slid wet over my bare back and when she dipped her hand under the water in my lap, I finally hissed and pushed back, hard enough to slide right out of the tub, landing in a crouch on the floor.

"Colette!" The older female spat the word out and Colette backed away, smirking. I stayed in a crouch, dripping on the floor as I backed away from both of them, looking for anything I could turn into a weapon. "Please child, let's just get you dressed," Rachel cajoled. Colette advanced, and I sprang at her. My attack surprised her and I landed a palm strike to her chest and a second to her face. She shrieked and lunged for me, but Rachel held her by the laces of her gown.

"I will kill you, witch," she hissed.

"No, you won't. Calm down, both of you." Rachel scolded us like we were in a schoolyard fight. She shoved Colette back. "Stop teasing Caroline, she's frightened." She held out her hand and I took it, not because she invaded me, but because I wanted her to keep protecting me from Colette.

"I just wanted to give her a kiss," the tiny vampire pouted. My hits had connected, and she'd barely blinked. I shuddered. I'd never been given the slightest attention from the males in my life. Now I was forced to protect my honor from a vampiress, just so her master could murder me for food.

I shuddered at the thought, but I was willing to die a thousand times as food rather than have Colette do what she suggested. Colette stalked toward me as though even thinking her name was a summons.

"I can be a very generous lover, pet," she spat at me as Rachel laced up the back of my low-cut dress. Rachel made a sound in her throat behind me and Colette stopped advancing.

"Perhaps your time is better served getting yourself ready for the master's awakening, Colette." Rachel led me over to a vanity and I sat on the bench seat in front of the mirror. She took my long, thick hair and wound it in an intricate style that piled on top of my head and left my neck and cleavage bare.

In the mirror, a very different me stared back from my reflection. Instead of looking younger, the up-style of my hair and plunging neckline of my bodice made me look older, more worldly and mature. I flushed at how much of me was visible and the pink spread quickly over my face and down to the ruffle that seemed the only thing preventing my breasts from escaping their bindings. A bell tolled in the distance and Rachel took my hand.

"It is time for the master to awake. You and the others will be good offerings." Others? My heart leapt at the thought that Becca and Mackenzie might still be alive. I let Rachel escort me down another long hall and clung to her for a moment when she stepped aside to let Colette take me through the door. "Don't worry, little one. She can't harm you. None of us can. You have been chosen for a most noble sacrifice." Another bell toll sounded in the distance and Colette took my hand and pressed me against her side, her lips against my ear.

"The master wakes, little witch." She held my face in her supernaturally strong hand and kissed my mouth, her lips tasting of mint and something metallic. I didn't fight her and she deepened the kiss. I concentrated all my strength, focus and will into my shield, until she yelped and jerked back. The force of my shield had driven her from me. White-faced, she glanced toward the room on the other side of the ornate door, hesitating. But the bell tolled a third time and the doors slowly opened in front of us.

The sexual sadist, Colette, gingerly placed my hand over her arm and walked me into a huge ballroom with the golden trappings and domed ceiling. I looked up at a mural above the crystal chandeliers, a horrific scene of blood and slaughter. Colette led me to the far end of the room where a coffin stood next to a throne. My heart raced as I stared at the ornate stone in front of me, mesmerized by my terrible fantasies of what lay inside.

Chapter 7

A sound caught my attention. I whipped my head around and saw two other girls being led into the room by other vampires. I recognized Becca not by any physical feature, but from the blank, glassy stare of the girl trailing behind her, barely able to hold up her own head. "Mackenzie", I thought to myself. She was a Renfield in truth and my heart ached for the pretty, vacant blonde and her frightened friend.

They were dressed as I was, in dresses that bared enough neck, cleavage, and arm to provide multiple places for a vampire to bite. Becca was tall, and athletic, and Mackenzie was even shorter and tinier than I was. It seemed that our master vampire didn't have a specific type that interested him as food, but rather that the vampires that took us had their own preferences. I watched the vampire leading Becca shoot possessive and territorial looks around the room as he walked her to her place and backed away to join Colette.

I didn't recognize any vampire power present as the one who took me. But, I tried to take in as much of the room as possible in the little glances I dared before the casket pulled my eyes back to it. The air in the huge room shifted and the fifty or so vampires that surrounded us stood at attention.

A vampire stepped out onto the dais from behind the throne and my blood curdled. I hadn't seen his face in the darkness when he took me, but the power that pressed against me like a physical weight was all too familiar. He was dressed like the others, in a cross between high Victorian fashion and an Anne Rice novel.

His boots came above his knees. Tight leather pants that laced up the front were tucked into them. His shirt was blood red and flowing and though it also laced up, it was undone in a deep "V" that showed the stark whiteness of his chest, a white made purer from lack of blood. His long black hair was slicked back and tied in a ponytail at the nape of his neck, making it appear, from the front, as though it cut close to the head. His eyes were a blue so pale they looked like small crystals of ice in an otherwise marble face. Looking at him was more terrifying than staring at the coffin, so that was where I focused. I only glancing at him from time to time as he began some sort of ritual.

He raised his hands and the crowd around us began chanting in unison. I took Becca's hand and focused on my shield, pulling all my reserves and shoving them into that feeling in my head I was beginning to recognize as my power.

"All praise the Master of the City, my brother, Nicholas, who is risen from his decades of slumber to lead us once more!" Vittorio, the pale vampire raised his voice and the vampires chanted louder with him. My blood froze in my veins at the sound, and I focused on not fainting from fear.

Becca moaned in anguish and I glanced up to see her friend being led by the hand to the dais. He stood her over the closed casket and from it tugged a needle into view. She stared unseeing ahead of her, as her slammed the needle into her arm at the soft spot inside her elbow, and I cringed and looked away as the room spun around me. I felt my hand being yanked and my shoulder almost dislocated as the vampire behind Becca moved forward to force her up to the other side of the casket.

I took a step toward her, but Colette grabbed my arm and pulled me back against her, so close that I could feel her heart race. She was afraid and her fear was enough to make me obey her without fighting. The vampire leading Becca stared into her eyes and her next scream died on her lips as her face went slack and the intelligence disappeared from her eyes.

A second needle was produced and both girls were drained, right in front of me. I dug my fingernails into my palms in disgust and shame. I'd been unable to save myself let alone the others kidnapped with me. They stayed standing long after I thought they would, swaying on their feet as the ruby liquid flowed from them into the casket.

As the two escorts finally picked up their charges and carried them out of sight, they were replaced by two more male vampires, who strained to lift the heavy stone lid and set it on the floor at the head of the coffin. They reached their hands in and I pressed harder against Colette. She didn't make any wisecracks and I was grateful. I wished for the magic ability to make myself invisible and slide right through her and the wall at her back. I held my breath as they lifted their master from his bed and it escaped in a loud whoosh as he turned and faced the room.

The sheer power that flowed out through the room nearly bowled me over as it slammed into my chest and pushed through me. Colette held me upright and when his gaze turned to us, she put my hand over her arm and led me up the steps to face him. The vampire that had first captured me hissed slightly and Colette glared at him before stepping between us. I felt the animosity between them, but I had eyes only for the master. Instead of a gnarled, ugly creature, I was staring at possibly the most handsome creature I had ever seen. His eyes were dark and green, like emeralds over onyx, and were deep set under heavy eyebrows. He was too rugged to be pretty, but his full lips, deep red from the blood that had just infused his body, softened the edges of the angles of his face. All the same, his power rang out in my head like a deep, clear bell. He was older than I had the ability to even guess.

The only visible physical imperfection was a long, ragged scar that ran from the corner of his right eye, down his cheek to his jaw. It was angry and red, but instead of ruining his face it managed to make him more handsome.

"Oh, shit. He's in my head," I thought to myself. Instantly, I felt two reactions. Colette, who I recognized, replied with something akin to "No kidding, stupid," while a second reaction of silent amusement merely tested my wall, gently prodding it while never taking his eyes from me. Angry and scared, I slapped at him. His eyes widened a split second before his power rammed through me like a

Mac truck. I flew backward and landed hard on the stone floor, too stunned to even hit with my hands first. My head slammed against the floor right after my shoulders and the earth shook.

Hands lifted me up. I kept my eyes closed as much from the pain as from the fear of what was holding me. I trembled and a flicker of annoyance passed through him, as I felt him force his way into my thoughts again. I knew the master had me pinned against him, his mouth hovering over my throat. My walls had crumbled. In a final effort to at least die as me, instead of a mindless zombie, I repeated the Latin spell I had memorized from Dominique's book aloud. It was the one she had begun to teach in class to chase intruders from our psyches.

It didn't force him out, but he paused and instead of pushing harder, he picked me up and cradled me in his arms. I risked opening my eyes and once the stars cleared I was looking up at a face still impossibly beautiful. That I was so attracted to him wasn't glamor, at least not consciously. "Oh God," I thought to myself. "David's ability to draw women *is* a psychic gift." The thought made me groan aloud and the master vampire looked down at me in alarm. I closed my eyes and made myself as small as I could wishing that he'd forget me.

"Not likely, little one. You are far too sweet for me to simply forget I have you in my arms," he chuckled, his voice deep and thick as taffy. I stiffened and he laughed again. It was a masculine chuckle that sounded very much alive and stirred things I would never have expected deep in my stomach. My pulse fluttered and I felt a masculine sense of triumph in him.

He set me down in a chair by a fire, in a bedroom of sorts. There were books all around me, stacked on the floor, the tables, and on shelves that lined almost every wall. The large, four-poster bed that stood to one side was bigger than any king sized I'd ever seen. The room itself was richly decorated, with heavy red drapes covering the windows. The tapestries hanging on the walls depicted hunting scenes with hounds and men on horses chasing a fox through the woods and over pastures.

I was so taken with the room, I forgot to be afraid of the master himself and smiled as I pulled a small hill of books into my lap and held them like baby birds, cradled in my hands.

"Are these all yours?" I gasped.

"One does tend to gather things, when one lives long enough," he drawled. I gaped at him, astonished at how quickly I'd forgotten he was the big bad wolf I feared. His glamour was powerful, but impossible to detect if I wasn't concentrating on it. My heart thudded in my chest. He held up a hand to dismiss my thoughts. "I'm not going to harm you. Despite whatever you may have heard or been taught, we are not animals."

"Oh, I'm quite sure that some of you are." I pictured the photo I kept by my bed, of my mother and father.

"Just as you have monsters among you, so do we." He held out a hand, and though I tried to fight it, my hand slid into his. I was surprised to find it warm and strong, and too pleasant to admit to myself. He released my hand abruptly as Rachel appeared with a tray in her hands. I smelled Lady Grey tea as she set a filigreed cup next to my elbow and another by the master's.

"You and your kind are sharks. You exist only to prey on humans. Just because you are beautiful, doesn't mean you're good," I argued, but my voice sounded unsure and weak.

"Watch your tongue," warned Rachel sharply. The master raised his hand and she bit off her next words. At his dismissal, she left us alone again.

"Who are you?" I asked, fighting to keep my voice cool and sure, despite the turmoil in my gut and the ringing in my head from the blow it had taken.

"Ah, Miss Caroline," he replied. I nodded and lifted the teacup he pushed toward me. "I am Nicholas. I am most pleased to make the acquaintance of a young Venatores with such distinguishing power," he added. "Dominique has taught you well, but you are so very young." His voice trailed off as he watched me flinch in surprise before I could school my expression blank. "Oh, yes, the Borgia family and I go back beyond ages."

"You read my mind," I said accusingly. He nodded. His face was inscrutable and it made me more anxious than if I knew what he felt. If he felt anything at all. "Are you going to drain me?" I couldn't stop the words from flowing out of my mouth, even as I saw the flicker of irritation in his face.

"Perhaps." I gulped hard. I needed to keep him wanting me alive more than dead.

"Lady Borgia is one of our greatest sorceresses, but she is very mysterious. If you were from a family that had been assassins for a thousand years, you would be mysterious too," he retorted, one corner of his mouth lifting in amusement.

I gasped. I had heard rumors, but that they were true was thrilling. I suddenly had more questions than I thought anyone but Dominique herself could answer.

"How, do you know Lady Borgia?"

"Even in the beginning, the Borgias were wealthy aristocrats and patrons of the arts. They were also always aware that another world thrived beneath the cover of darkness. Our relationship was mutually beneficial." I cringed. The master vampire was friends with the sorceress who was training me to kill vampires, had possibly killed for her own family.

"Kill me, or let me go," I demanded. I couldn't believe the Venatores capable of working with vampires. I refused to listen to a master vampire's lies.

"You don't get to make demands," he snarled. "I will keep you as I wish, let you live, or let you die. For now, you're interesting to me. Do not assume that we kill as easily as your beloved hunters. The Venatores are far more bloodthirsty than we have ever been, yet your tiny sect still exists, does it not?"

"You're saying you could kill us all, if you wished?"

"We obey the laws our elders and the Venatores set before us. But, yes, if it came to war, there would be no Venatores Lamiae left."

"You work with the hunters?"

He smiled at me, a predatory grin that made my pulse race and my mouth dry. "Those I find intriguing," he replied, glancing down at the pulse fluttering in my throat. "You, my dear naïve little Caroline, are most intriguing."

I looked away and stared into the fire as it danced and blazed, warming my face. Slowly it dawned on me that the fire and the tea were for my benefit. A master vampire wouldn't have need of a flame. The room, the fire, it was mine, not his. I wasn't going to die. Not tonight, anyway. I sipped my tea and thought. If I wasn't dead yet, I just had to live until sunrise.

I hummed over my teacup and built up my shield around me, one thought as a time. I had no intention of dying. I had to make it back to the Venatores. I had no idea which way was up anymore, but I did know that I had questions, and they were going to give me answers.

I glanced over at the master vampire but his seat was empty. I was chilled. his power to cloud my mind was so expert that he had left without me noticing. My bravado fled and I shivered despite the roaring fire in front of me. I was alive, but all I had was questions and the stark terror of my reality. I was trapped and if he was telling me the truth, it was possible no one cared that I'd been taken.

Chapter 8

I couldn't begin to imagine going to sleep and when I tried the door and the windows, they were locked tight. I hadn't expected any less, but it was still disheartening to feel so helpless and alone.

I had been spoon fed hatred of vampires all my life. Now I had more questions about the Venatores Lamiae than I did about vampires. In fact, I had one question about vampires. How the hell did I get away from them and back home?

I missed David. The sting of his callous behavior had dulled in the face of what I was sure was my inevitable death by draining. My mind reached out for him. I'd never been away from him in my whole life since my parents died. He would never be my boyfriend. But, he was still my best friend.

Now, I was in the most terrifying of strange places, and David was a comforting weight in my mind. It was almost like he wasn't as far away as I feared. I reached out, but while I felt him, he wasn't close enough to respond, or maybe he didn't want to. I tried to do the same with Clayton, but we'd never been as close, and I couldn't feel him at all.

Feeling David meant that my mind wasn't invaded or under the effects of glamour. I ran to a window and threw back the curtains, expecting to see daylight, but there was complete black behind the glass. Frustrated, I examined it more closely, bringing the candelabra from the table closer to see better. The candles appeared in mirror image in the glass, aside my pale, frightened face and wide eyes. There was no view to the outside: only more stone, or dirt. Something kept the window from ever encountering the sunlight. I checked the remaining three windows and they were all the same. I slammed down the candle holder and screamed my frustration.

Despair overtook me easily as I sat in the corner of the room, my back to the wall. I hugged my knees to my chest and rocked, my mind refusing to accept any coherent thought that could help me out of my opulent prison. I thought of Domonique and the hunters. My questions required that I live to receive answers.

I breathed in and counted to eight as I exhaled, like I had learned to do to control my anxiety. As I worked on my breathing, I realized I hadn't thought of anxiety or depression since I'd been taken. Apparently fight or flight responses trumped garden-variety issues. Either that or the master's glamour was affecting my unconscious responses.

With that thought in mind, I practiced my mental shield, putting up and removing the wall repeatedly until I could do it without focusing on each individual part. I wished that I had Dominique's book with me so I could practice spells. I hadn't read the whole thing. It was possible a spell that could immobilize vampires was sitting in my carry-on in my hotel room while I was wondering how many hours of life I had left.

I reached out with my mind, sending tendrils of thought through the stone and spreading them like fingers down the corridors, trying to sense vampires. As I searched, my brain kept going back to David. My fledgling talent honed in on him instead of vampires, snapping together as one bolt of psychic energy. The energy poured into another room in the ancient building. He was closer than I could've imagined and I could feel his terrible pain even though he wasn't conscious or responding to me.

The scream that tore out of my throat was like the shriek of a wounded animal. I was pulled inside him, and wasn't strong or in control enough to get out. I was caged, feeling every laceration and broken bone like they were my own.

My wails continued after Rachel rushed into the room and I was aware of being moved as she carried me to the bed. Suddenly, the pain started to go away, until it disappeared completely. Shaking and covered in frigid sweat, I opened my eyes to see dark green eyes fringed in impossibly black lashes, staring back at me.

"You're in shock," the master said softly, laying a heavy blanket over me and tucking it under me so I was pinned to the bed. "Can you speak?" I cleared my throat, raw and swollen from my screams.

"I don't know what happened," I whimpered, my voice full of gravel from pain and emotion. He pressed his hand against my forehead and I glanced over at Rachel. It surprised me that her face was pinched with worry.

"What were you doing before you were attacked?" I stiffened. "Nothing you say will bring you harm."

"I was trying to control my, my fear, and use Lady Borgia's training," I whispered, pausing as a harsh cough tore at my throat and lungs. "But, I don't have her notes anymore, so I could only practice what I have memorized." My breathing was steadier now and I noticed that the tight covers had warmed me quickly and slowed my shaking. I tried to sit up and after a moment's hesitation, the master sat back enough so that I could pull myself up against the pillows.

"Then what happened, tiny hunter?" he coaxed. His voice was gentle, but his smirk made it more teasing, less compassionate.

"I tried exploring. I was thinking about my friend and suddenly I could feel him and everything in me aimed straight toward hm. I felt like I was inside him, trapped inside his broken body, stabbed, chained. It was the worst pain I could've imagined and then some. I was helpless." He glanced at Rachel, who shrugged and shook her head.

"Rest. I will be back soon." Nicholas stood up and strode toward the door. I felt the emptiness in the depression he'd left on the bed. The feeling of loss was crushing and I erected my psychic shield to protect me from the love-glamour that surrounded him like an aura.

I'd begun to believe his glamour was unintentional and maybe automatic, but that made it no less compelling. My top priority in getting out of here alive had to be becoming strong enough to resist that pull.

Chapter 9

"Where did the master, Nicholas, go?" I asked Rachel. She shot me a sideways look and continued stoking the fire. "I'm afraid Rachel. Please help me. The pain was so real. How is that possible?" She made a sound of disgust and pointed at the chair in front of the slowly growing flames. I slunk over to the chair, watching for her to attack, but she went back to ignoring me until I was seated. Another blanket, lighter than the last, was flung over me and tucked in at my sides, covering me to my waist but leaving everything above it free to move.

"Of course it felt real, you little idiot," she sighed. "What on earth are those Venatores teaching you young ones these days?"

I stammered and coughed. I had never heard anyone speak of the society of hunters except in reverence. Hearing her sound frustrated made her seem more human than monster. I didn't know how to feel about my sworn enemies acting almost like regular people.

"Nothing, yet. I'm just a student, I haven't graduated to an apprenticeship yet." She made another sound of exasperation and set a teacup down hard enough that hot tea splashed into the saucer.

"What you were describing was astral projection, my dear. Most humans don't have a talent like that, even psychics. Most vampires don't either. If it was a lie to distract the master, you will suffer for it." She sighed and fluffed pillows, glaring at them like their lack of bouncy fullness was a personal affront.

"You don't think I was lying!" I argued. My body was warm and comforted by the fire and the tea, but inside me, there was a core of cold iron that fought against the creature comforts.

"You went into shock. I haven't been on this side of the veil so long that I don't remember what that means to a person." I chewed my lip as I watched her tidy the piles around me, as if she was burning off nervous energy.

"Why don't you hate me?" I blurted.

"You aren't my enemy. I would no more hate you than a helpless piglet in a pen," she scoffed.

"Does the master see me as food?" I pressed. The idea that I was livestock made my stomach churn unpleasantly around the tea.

"Blood is our food. Not people. Unlike most of you humans, the greater majority of us don't kill to eat. Now. No more questions. Just, sit quietly and wait until the master returns." Rachel returned to tidying without talking to me.

"Please, sit with me?" I asked. My brain was screaming at me to stay away from her, fight her, and protect myself. But her actions and those of the master, made me question my own hatred.

The Venatores had secrets, that much I understood. But the ease with which the master had spoken of them, of the laws they shared, seemed an unlikely lie. Besides, lying to me seemed like a waste of time. Rachel sat in the chair next to me. Her body was so still, it was impossible to mistake her for a human. There was a quality to the stillness that made my heart pound and my lungs seize and I fought to control my reaction.

"Why are you suddenly so afraid?" she asked. Her voice was normal, without power or glamour in it.

"You seem so, human, I forgot to be afraid of you, and that scared me more than I was before." Rachel laughed, an unexpected coarse, raucous sound that startled me almost out of my chair.

"Who told you to be afraid of me?" she asked, her voice condescending.

"I don't know, aren't most humans afraid of the undead? Even the ones who don't know vampires really exist?"

She stared into my eyes long enough that my bravado failed me, and I was the first to look away. When I glanced back at her, she was looking away, as though listening to something in the distance. When she saw me watching, she smiled at me gently.

"The master returns shortly," she reported and I tried to ignore the bump in my pulse. "Would you like me to tell you how I came to be here, like this, while we wait on him?" I nodded and she continued. "I am young for a vampire, though I was older when I was turned," she began, cupping her cheek in her hand. "That's why I look older than the master," she sighed. "I was hit by a drunk driver while walking home with my sister," she said. I swallowed hard and my bottom lip tucked between my teeth as I listened.

"What happened?" I asked when she didn't continue. Her face was sad, almost teary. It struck me that she chose to exhibit her feelings even though she didn't have to. She liked her humanity.

"My sister died instantly, but I didn't know that at the time," she replied. My chest tightened for her and I shifted to see her better while she spoke. "I was bleeding, holding her hand, when the most handsome man approached. He bent over my sister first, then touched my wounds and felt my heartbeat."

"The master?" I asked. She nodded.

"He leaned in and whispered to me, saying that I didn't have to die. That he could save me, if I wished. I thought he meant both of us and I agreed readily."

"And when you awoke?"

"I was starving. If I had happened upon a human being, I would have torn them to shreds like a rabid bear." I shuddered, thinking about my own family.

"Did you?" my voice betrayed emotion where I meant to hide it.

"No. I had Nicholas to teach me. I was the last he turned before it was his time to sleep."

"How long ago was that?"

"The masters sleep every five hundred years, for fifty. They take their strength from their coven and their hibernation slows the decay of their bodies."

"How many times has he done this?" I gasped, leaning toward her.

"You witnessed his third awakening." I fell back into my chair. Fifteen *hundred* years, he'd been a vampire, the living dead.

"That doesn't give me a reason not to fear you."

"Oh, I don't mind you fearing us. You are weak and ignorant. But the master is not a monster and we are quite civilized, once you know our ways."

"But, your kind murder people for food."

"Oh, do we? And how would you know that?"

"Rachel." The voice was low and stern. Rachel blinked slowly, then stood.

"Master."

"Tend to Colette. She is injured. And treat the boy. He needs to be ready to be sent back to his people." My pulse skyrocketed.

"Wait, the boy? David? Is he here? I need to see him." I was out of my chair and at the door faster than even I thought possible, and Nicholas apparently agreed, as he lunged after me and threw me back on the bed with a hiss.

"Kill me, or let me go to him. I won't stop trying to reach him." I slid off the bed onto my feet and braced for a blow from his raised hand.

"Damnit, girl." He nodded to Rachel, who bowed and left the room without a sound. "He is in no shape for company right now. You will see him when Rachel has had time to see to his wounds."

"Oh, my God. How badly is he wounded?" Tears stung my eyelids.

"Badly enough that I would advise against another round of astral projection into his body." Nicholas turned to go without another word.

"How long am I to be alone in here? What are you going to do to me?" I called out to his retreating back. His shoulders slumped in a very human gesture and he glanced back over his shoulder.

"I have to deal with some coven business. I will return shortly. If you haven't used the bath in the adjoining room, do so, and be ready to eat when I return."

He slipped out the door and I heard the sharp click of the key in the lock before I was once again alone in silence. I tried the door, halfheartedly, but it was locked tight, as I expected. I heard running water from the other room and entered to find more of the lush bath towels Rachel had used on me when she had dressed me for the awakening.

I dragged a chair to the door and shoved it under the latch, to hold the door shut. It wouldn't stop a vampire, I knew, but at least it would make enough noise that I couldn't be surprised. Wishing I'd thought of it sooner, I slipped into the en-suite and did the same with the door that lead from the bedroom to the corridor.

David had been taken too. My heart broke for his pain, possibly even caused by an attempt to save me. I shut off the water wondering how an old stone building not only had running water, but heated too. "Vampires bathe too, I guess," I thought to myself as I added a handful of the fragrant soap flakes Rachel had used before. After one last check of both doors I finally undressed.

The hot water soothed my aching muscles and started to finally warm the icy center of me, where my contact with David had made me feel almost hypothermic from the sudden agony of his wounds, both physical and psychological. Part of me prayed that David had simply been caught away from the crowds of the resort and that I had no responsibility for the state he was in. But there was that selfish core of me that hoped he'd fought to get to me and been taken as a result.

"And you say we're monsters?" A sly voice scoffed from the corner of the room. I gasped and splashed as I tried to see Colette, glancing all around me for something

I could use as a weapon. "Oh, I'm not going to hurt you, but only because the master forbids it. You stole my new toy, Caroline. I'm very cross with you."

Past the pounding of my heart, I realized her voice was in my head, not in the room with me. Strangely, knowing she wasn't physically in the room while I was naked was more comforting than worrisome. She was nuts, and too powerful to keep out of my head. Better that though, than her hands on me again. Even so, I finished my bath quickly and when I heard the chair fall away from the bedroom door, with a rather satisfying crash, I was dried and dressing.

"Really, Caroline. Must you?" Rachel's exasperated voice floated in from the bedroom. Despite myself, I giggled, pulling the dress up over my shoulders

"Sorry, Rachel. But with Colette in my head the way she was, I wasn't taking any chances with being caught off guard."

Rachel peeked into the bathroom and motioned for me to turn around so she could tighten the laces at the back.

"She had David. She was the one torturing him." My voice cracked and my hands fisted at my sides. For a split-second I hoped Colette could hear my thoughts, see the death I had in mind for her, for beating and bleeding David.

"It appears that way. That lost soul was physically and emotionally tortured by her own father. The vampire that changed her did so to make her harder to kill, so she could survive worse. He then violated her in every way imaginable and more frequently than he could were she human. She healed every physical injury he gave her. But, her sanity was hanging by a thin thread. The horrors he visited upon her, physically and sexually, caused irreparable emotional damage."

"So, Nicholas wasn't her maker. Can he stop her?" Rachel sat me at the vanity so she could squeeze more water out of my hair and brush it.

"Colette has sworn a blood oath of fealty to Nicholas. He loves her like a cherished sister and she loves him. She could no more hurt you, than hurt Nicholas himself, unless he wishes it." She sighed and placed her hands on my shoulders. "But, you must focus on your safety. Obey the master. No more demands. He's patient, but only so far." I clenched my hands in small, white fists in my lap, but said nothing.

I looked up at her. Her face never changed from the pleasant blank she'd perfected as a serving woman to her master, perhaps even before. But her hands stayed busy, even when they accomplished nothing.

Perhaps the master would be pleased enough to let us go, if I was obedient like Rachel had warned. I stood and twirled in the center of the stone floor, the voluminous skirt of my Victorian dress billowing out around me. It was beautiful and despite everything that had happened, I felt a tiny spark of satisfaction in my appearance.

I started searching the bookshelves and piles of books for something to teach me what the school had failed to. I needed to learn about my captors. When I reached the fireplace and the ancient, leather-bound books stacked next to and between the chairs, I had a small mountain stacked in my arms.

I created a new pile next to the chair by the fire and moved the stacks that were there already back towards the bookshelves. I had almost finished setting myself up my reading pile, when I noticed a folded leather envelope, tied with a cord.

I unwrapped the leather and laid it flat, whistling under my breath at the yellowed parchment inside. The handwriting was eerily familiar and very quickly I could see that I was looking at the same spells Dominique had given me. My heart lurched as I tried to wrap my head around how old Dominique really was.

I reread the spells that were still legible, but the ink on the others had faded past the point of usefulness. Those I set aside. If Nicholas had kept notes from his friend for so many hundreds of years, perhaps he had read and memorized them.

I arranged my dress as comfortably as I could and sat to read while I waited for some news of David, or the other girls who were taken. The old spells and psychic practices were a comfort to read, but made me think about the parallels between my life and the lives that my captors lived in. They were the 'big bad', the monster in the closet, the ultimate evil in the world. But now, more and more, it seemed that they were very much like the hunters.

Poor Rachel seemed like a nice person who had kept her humanity locked somewhere inside her. Even Colette was not just some empty predator. She had a history, a dark and tortured past that made her who she was. Nicholas was well over a thousand years old, and so powerful that none of his coven questioned him or how he dealt with them. The civility that I had been treated with was a jarring contradiction to the way I had been taken and what had been done to David.

The contradictions weren't helping my crisis of faith. In my heart, I knew the vampires weren't the scourge I'd been taught. Or at least, that's not all they were. Maybe the hunters weren't as pure as I'd thought, either.

I set aside the sheaf of papers and paced the room, thinking, until Rachel informed me that I had been summoned to dine with the master. My mind immediately filled with images of poor, defenseless people stretched across banquet tables like so much meat and I shuddered. She stepped forward as I hesitated and held out a hand.

"He's done nothing to bring you harm, Caroline. Don't let your prejudices put you on the wrong side of his temper and your time here will be pleasant." Her phrasing, "your time here" gave me the small hope that David and I could still leave here together.

I nodded and followed her out the door, congratulating myself on my bravery as bloody imaginings filled my head with every step.

Chapter 10

The banquet hall was empty but for a long table surrounding by high-back, velvet cushioned chairs. At one end, there were candles and place settings for two. Vampires in the white uniforms of servants followed me in, placing fragrant platters of chicken and baked bread on the table before exiting silently. My mouth watered at the sight and smell of the feast in front of me.

My pulsed jumped at the realization that I was to be alone with the master. But at the same time, I was relieved that not only was I not going to be on the menu, I wouldn't be forced to watch the monsters feed. Rachel pulled back my chair and briefly touched my shoulder, then left me alone. The candles guttered and chills went down my spine, as I tried to see into the shadows just beyond their light.

I was feeling the effects of a full day without sleep and reached for the glass in front of me, hoping to feel more refreshed with some water. It was a shock when the fruity tang of wine hit my lips instead and I choked a little on the liquid as it went down my throat.

"Miss Caroline. I hope you have found the accommodations to your liking, despite your earlier mishap." Nicholas' voice was suddenly at my shoulder and I gasped and froze. If it was possible, he was taller and more imposing by the candlelight of the banquet hall than he had been when first awakened. Pride, more than bravery, guided my nod of response. Watching him was like seeing a big cat at the zoo and realizing the glass between you had disappeared. I stayed very still, watchful and quiet. He stared back at me with eyes that appeared black and bottomless in the flickering light and my pulse sped further.

"Don't you approve of the accommodations?" he asked. His face was unreadable, but his voice held amusement.

"I would feel better about it if I hadn't just found out my fellow hunter was bleeding and broken. Is he going to be okay?" Nicholas sighed.

"He is in pain, but he will live."

"I have to see him for myself. I'm sure you understand."

"You're very demanding for one in your position," he growled. His voice was low and calm, but the undercurrent of anger raised the hair on my neck.

"Please, I apologize for offending you and you have provided me with everything I have needed since I was ta— since I arrived. But, even you were worried when you saw me in that kind of pain. I can't pretend I'm a guest at a party after that," I pleaded with him.

"I understand that you will not be able to enjoy a meal until you have made certain we did not kill him," he sighed again. "Eat what you can stomach, to regain your strength and I will show you the darker delights of my kingdom, if you have the stomach for it." The look in his eyes when he said "delights", made my stomach quake. Still, I forced a few forkfuls of food down, trying not to look like a cow with him watching me.

He stood and offered me his hand when he was satisfied I'd had enough, and led me through the kitchen down stairs to part of the building that reminded me of my first prison cell.

"Why was David here?" I asked, after a minute of uncomfortable silence. Being quiet with Nicholas was not like the quiet between two humans. When he was quiet, there was nothing to indicate he was there. No footsteps or breathing. Even his clothes moved silently as he walked and the silence filled me with dread.

"Vampires who begin as humans keep all their predilections of their former life. Just as the two females who awakened me are likely to remain a couple, vampires usually have a strong opinion of which gender they prefer to feed from."

"So David was brought to be food for someone other than you?"

"He was chosen, along with other males and females to be here for anyone who needed them. What happened to him was unfortunate. The rest of the donors have already been returned to their homes, with no recollection of what happened to them."

"And the other two girls from your awakening?"

"To awaken me, we needed to drain them to the point of death. It's an honor to be chosen to be the first new children of a master when he wakes. It takes a trusted lieutenant to make the choice. A matter I left to my brother, Vittorio, whom you have met." I shuddered inwardly and hoped he didn't notice. Vittorio had *taken* me. "Introduction" was too kind a word to use for kidnapping.

"So, I'm alive because I didn't make the cut?" I scoffed, but inwardly felt torn between relief and being offended. I had no desire to be a vampire. But the attention Nicholas had given me made me feel more important than I ever had.

"You would have fed me, if I wished it," he replied. "I wanted to learn from you." My feet stopped moving and I stared up at him, wishing I could read his thoughts as he so freely did mine. I didn't understand what I saw in his eyes, but my heart fluttered in my chest and for a moment it was hard to breathe.

"What could I possibly teach you?" I asked, hoping the dark hid the hot blush I felt in my cheeks. He laughed gently and tugged me into motion again, placing his hand over mine on his arm.

"I have been asleep for fifty years, seeing only what my coven saw in the night. When I entered your mind, I learned about what has changed in the daylight. How people have changed, social orders, fads, and technology. But, I desire to hear you talk about it all."

"You care about technology?" I asked, incredulous.

"Why does that surprise you so much? What else does an immortal creature have to keep them from going mad, but curiosity about the evolution of the world around them?"

I nodded, thinking ahead, at the end of whatever he thought I could show him.

"Will I get to go home?" I bit my lip and looked straight ahead at the stairs ahead. I balked at descending them, even though it was a wider and less daunting staircase than the one I had ascended from my first prison cell here.

"That is not for you to worry about, yet. I expect you to be more compliant after you are assured of your friend's prognosis."

I glanced sideways up at him, his dark hair curling on the high collar of his shirt, an emerald green silk that matched his eyes. I was heading toward David, the boy I had spent most of my life half in love with, and now I couldn't stop being distracted by this man who was so self-assured and powerful. He had nothing to prove to anyone and it was my company he wanted.

He stopped before a door guarded by one of the male vampires who had opened Nicholas' coffin at the awakening. He too bowed and backed away. My pulse thumped as Nicholas opened the door and motioned me through.

At first I stayed close to the wall, searching the room visually and with my mind for any other vampires. All I found was a bed at the end of the room and in it, my friend, his skin as pale as the sheets under him with blooms of black and purple bruises on his face and arms. I was sure if I lifted the light coverlet that lay over him, I would find more of the same down his abdomen and legs.

The swelling in his face forced one eye shut, but he glared at me from the other until I came closer and he recognized me. His eye went wide with fear and something else I couldn't identify.

"David, what did they do to you?" I rushed to his side, unable to hold back the tears that flooded down my cheeks. I was trembling as I touched his shoulders as gently as I could. "I tried to find an escape and instead I found you." He closed his eye and I sat back and sobbed into my hands. "I felt your wounds," I confessed, tears sliding down my cheeks. "I felt your pain and it was the worst thing I have ever endured."

I felt his bandaged hand over my own, and wiped my eyes on my sleeve so I could see him properly. He tugged at my hand, moving his lips like he was talking. I leaned in, placing my ear next to his mouth.

"You're warm." I sniffed and chuckled.

"I'm still me." I felt his body relax next to me on the bed. "The vampire that did this to you. She terrifies me." His head shook slightly, and his mouth and throat worked as he tried to swallow. A glass of water appeared at my hand and I held it to David's lips, letting him draw in small sips until he nodded and pulled away.

"There was a girl. But she didn't do this." He held up his bandaged hands. "I remember her. She said her name was Colette. She was on a path that led to the beach." He closed his eye, his breathing shallow. "Clayton. He was right behind me, I don't know if he's alive." He sniffed, and I wiped his nose with a corner of the bedsheet. "She fed on me. It was like nothing I've ever experienced, like sex but better," David told me, his voice raspy. I scoffed.

"I'll have to take your word for it." He managed a weak smile through his cracked, dry lips. "Of course. Of all the people who have been taken, you were too special to be food."

"Don't. Not now. I have no idea what will happen to me. "I ignored the leaden fear in the pit of my stomach. "Did you tell them you were a hunter in training?" He frowned.

"I don't remember what I said at first. I invoked the Venatores when the male took me and bound me. It was like I was drugged, too high to argue or fight back."

"There were two vampires?" I asked, confused.

"In the beginning, there was just the girl. Then the male came and he bound me. They fought and he took me and beat me up. I didn't see the girl again until just before he came." David pointed at Nicholas. "There are at least twenty of them, Caroline. We're going to die here."

"Hey, now. This is the master, Nicholas. He promised to get you back to the school as soon as you were well enough. Can you sit up?" He let me assist him into a half-upright position against the pillows. Nicholas stepped forward and bowed at the neck at David.

"I will leave you to your reunion. Caroline, when you're finished, come to me. Your friend needs time alone to rest. He'll be safe here. I nodded and watched him go, wishing I'd thanked him for saving David and letting me see him.

"What about you?" David asked as I watched Nicholas leave. I slowly turned back to him, a strange feeling in my stomach.

"I will do my part and hope I get to leave too." I gave him a weak smile.

"You really felt my pain." I nodded. "I felt you, too. I thought it was the vampire, until I heard the scream and realized it wasn't me. Then I didn't know what to think." He stroked my finger. "I should never have left you alone."

"But, you did. And then you didn't try to find me after a pretty girl caught your eye," I said, my voice empty of emotion. "I thought you were my only true friend. I would have done anything for you." He closed his eye, his breathing shallow again, and I took a deep breath. He'd hurt me, but that was no excuse for attacking him now, while he lay there in pain. "David, I will do everything I can to get you home safely. Can I count on you to at least tell them I'm still here?" My voice broke and I breathed out a shaky sigh.

"We'll come back for you," he promised. I nodded, but my heart sank. I didn't believe him. I couldn't count on him to keep me safe, not anymore.

"If you don't, then I'll find a way on my own." I could see that he knew I had lost faith in him and anger flashed in his good eye.

"Hey, I'm in here, because of you. Why are you angry?" He blurted. I stood, shaken by his accusation.

"No. You're here because you thought with the wrong body part. I would never have gone off in the darkness alone. If you'd bothered to go to my room, you would've known something was wrong." I backed away another step, painful realization dawning in me. "I don't belong to you anymore, David. I love you and it's killing me to see you hurt. But, I'm done lying to myself, that you still care about me." I turned and ran headlong into Rachel. She held me upright, and led me away from the bed.

"Caroline, the master still waits on you for supper." She stroked my hair and held me tight for a moment. She whispered in my ear: "The first heartbreak is always the worst. Come child, your new master awaits."

"Oh, Rachel, I can't. I can't go to supper with him and share polite conversation while David lies in that bed." She held the door and I led the way through, shivering at the sheer quantity of vampire energy that hit me when I walked out into the inhabited hallway. They seemed to ignore me as they went about their business, but I felt each one in my head like notes in a melody and I knew that they were forever etched on my memory.

"It doesn't serve you to anger him, Caroline," she warned me. I nodded.

"I know. But, I'll take my chances. Please take me to my room."

Chapter 11

When I felt the hot angry wind blast through the bedroom door, throwing away the chair I'd put under the latch across the room, I had a split second to regret not listening to Rachel, before I felt icy fingers around my throat and stars began to dance in front of my eyes. As I was strangled to near unconsciousness, I felt another long-fingered hand slide down the front of me, slipping beneath my neckline and cupping my small breast in a bloodless hand.

The familiar, terrifying power of Vittorio, the vampire that had taken me, along with a new fear, bloomed in my heart. I would have preferred an eternity of torture at the hands of Nicholas, than one moment enduring the touch of the monster that held me. I grabbed at his hands, as frantic to get him out of my bodice as I was to stay conscious. I tried, but couldn't scream, and the only sound that emerged from me was a gurgling, bubbling whisper.

Just as the darkness began to seep in from the edges of my mind, I managed to reach out for Rachel, the only vampire I thought might come to my aid. For just a moment, his hand slipped, and I caught a ragged, gasping breath.

"Don't bother calling for help. No one can hear you," he whispered to me, clenching his hands tighter. I went limp and he released my throat and stood in front of me, staring down at me as I coughed and shook from fear. I was in trouble, but I was still conscious. It was a win for me and I searched the room for ways to exploit it. Near the fireplace were iron tools, but they were out of reach.

He grabbed the bodice of my gown and pulled me to a standing position. "I hate my brother's Victorian sensibilities, quite frankly. But, I do appreciate the ease of undressing a whore in a dress." He pointed one clawed finger and sliced through the fabric, and I felt a swift burning pain, followed by wetness, and I knew he'd drawn blood.

"Someone will stop you," I spat, shoving as hard as I could and rearing back to kick him in the knee as he held me inches above the floor. He slammed me up against the wall next to the fireplace. I kicked out wildly and spilled the set of tools, hoping they were close enough to grab if he dropped me. With one long arm, he grabbed the poker from the tools I'd scattered to the floor with my struggling and jammed it under the burning logs.

"Maybe, but not before I've had my fun," he hissed, spittle flying into my face. "Do you really believe my brother would choose you over me?" He yanked on my dress and it tore like paper, falling away from my chest and stomach while the remainder hung off my back by my sleeves. "Ask Colette, if she can speak when she's released from her coffin in a hundred years or so." His mouth was on my neck as his hands wandered over me and I felt the prick of his fangs breaking the skin, forcing a shriek of sheer terror from me as I pounded on him with impotent fists, kicking and screaming like a crazy person.

Suddenly, he dropped me in a pile on the floor. I wrapped my arms over my neck and curled my legs in to protect my soft parts, still screaming. When another blow never came, I dared to look around. Nicholas and the black-haired vampire were grappling on the other side of the room, and as I watched, the slender vampire danced away from the master and sliced at his face with his claws, drawing blood. I glanced down. The poker was still in the fire.

I grabbed it, not thinking, and my hand burned instantly from the heat of the handle. I forced myself to hold onto it, and staggered at them. I raised the poker as high as the agonizing pain would allow. I stabbed it into Vittorio's leg, high up on the back of his thigh. He yowled in pain and jerked away, taking the poker, and layers of skin from my hand, with him. Nicholas stood between us as I sagged to the floor. Nicholas motioned with his head and vampires flooded into the room and grabbed the other vampire by the arms and legs.

"Lock Vittorio in a cell," he ordered, straightening his jacket. "Make sure you take the poker out first." The male vampire closest to him nodded and yanked the poker out of Vittorio's thigh. I gasped as I realized how deep I'd managed to impale him. I only wished I'd been able to raise my arm to the level of his heart.

Rachel stayed behind when the others left and Colette was close behind her. Her face was tight and even paler than usual, if that was possible. It was Colette who examined my hand, blowing cool air across the raw, bloody skin and dancing to one side, as the pain made me vomit bile.

"Colette. You've only just been released. Do not make me put you back before you've had a chance to feed." She cringed and her eyes went to the floor.

"Her hand is so hot it hurts my skin. I was just trying to cool it." I glanced down at her, kneeling so she was smaller than me, my hand cupped in hers as in supplication.

"I'm okay. It just hurts so, so much." Colette glanced up at me, then at Nicholas.

"I can heal her," Colette said softly. Her face was paler than I'd seen; so translucent I could clearly see the veins below her skin.

"No, Colette. You may not." The master's voice was stern but not angry. She backed away from me and Rachel put her to work, righting the furniture and making the evidence of violence disappear before my eyes. I wished they could do the same with my hand, which had started trembling uncontrollably once Colette let go of it.

"Leave us!" Nicholas' bark startled all three of us equally and even as I cringed away from him, I saw Colette and Rachel draw back towards each other. "Stop cringing like beaten dogs and leave us, please," he added with a glance toward me. He held out his hand and I placed my good one in it, so he could help me to my feet.

"Are you angry with me?" I asked, my voice shaky and small.

"Not nearly as angry as I am with myself," he admitted. "You should have come down to supper with me."

"I wasn't hungry," I argued lamely.

"Yes, I know."

"He was... is, my foster brother." I paused and cleared my throat, then looked Nicholas in the eye. "His parents took me in, when a vampire murdered my parents. I was only three when it happened."

"I'm sorry to hear of your loss."

"A vampire tore their throats out and bled them dry while I sat in my crib, watching. Loss is not really an adequate word," I corrected. The combination of fear, anger, and pain had my system flooded with adrenaline.

". I understand your fear of us." He replied. "Your brother saved Colette. I should have asked him sooner who hurt him. Colette's thoughts can be difficult to interpret."

"Some people are monsters and so are *some* vampires. I'm learning. I've always wondered why the vampire didn't kill me too." I confessed.

"You are special. You have laughable control over your psychic ability, but your raw power is enough that you broke through a shield built to be strong enough to keep me out, and sensed your brother." He helped me up onto the bed and laid me back against the pillows, placing another one under my hand so it was elevated, palm up. "Perhaps you were able to make the vampire leave."

"Could I do it again?" My voice was clipped, and he looked at me sharply.

"I could train you to, yes." He sighed. "But first, I have to heal this. It could get infected and I need you healthy and whole." Something in his voice made me nervous and I tried to pull my hand back, but his hand shot out, lightning fast, and gripped me tight by the wrist.

"Please," I whimpered. He released my hand and leaned over me, his hand on my stomach.

"I'm not going to damage you, but this might sting." His hand slid up my bare stomach and over my breast and I gasped as pleasure surged through me, so different from what I had just experienced. I didn't have time to register embarrassment before his leg went between mine and he pinned me at my hip. He pressed down so I couldn't wriggle out from under him. His hand moved past my chest to my throat and chin, pushing my face away from him and baring my carotid artery.

"Oh God. Please, please don't," I whimpered and shook, the trembling intensifying as I felt his breath on my ear.

"I won't take enough to harm you, I simply need to feed before I can heal you. I promise. Everything I take I will return to you." His lips brushed my jaw and moved down to my neck and I fought the urge to pull him tighter to me. I felt torn between the pleasure of his closeness and the understanding that I was completely at the mercy of a creature that could take my life as easily as a thought.

There was a prick of fangs at my throat and his aura was so enthralling that all I desired was to give him everything he wanted. He chuckled and I crimsoned, realizing he was in my head Again. His laugh was enough to bring me back to myself a little, but the pain in my hand still made concentrating on a psychic shield too difficult.

Hit bit down and I understood what David had been trying to explain. Pleasure rushed through me to places that I had never been touched. My hand clutched at him, holding him to me even as I begged him to stop. He moaned into my shoulder and licked over the place where he'd bitten me.

"I sealed the wound. No need to worry about bleeding," he explained as he pushed up off me and I felt my throat for punctures. I could feel the two pinpricks, but my hand came away clean of anything but some saliva. He rolled up his sleeve past the wrist and sliced his skin open with one fingernail. I balked and pushed away, the euphoria of his bite replaced by revulsion.

"You can't expect me to..."

"Drink. It will heal your hand. I told you I would return what was yours." I gagged and shook my head. "You enjoyed it when I took it, I felt your body respond to me, even if I hadn't heard your thoughts. Taking it from me will produce a similar rush. That's how we get repeat donors," he whispered. He lifted me and held me with my back against him. "Please let me heal you." He lifted the narrow red stripe to my mouth and I flicked my tongue over it to gauge my gag reflex.

The tiny hit of his power on my tongue felt like I'd licked an electrical socket, if doing such a thing could make you high and aroused. I latched on to him and drew my tongue over him, using it to pry into the wound he'd made and then sinking my teeth into the flesh around it to push more blood out to my waiting mouth. I felt him grow aroused, pressing into my rear, and for one heart-stopping moment I realized where the exchange could lead. Then I was alone. His wrist was gone from my mouth and when I glanced around, I saw the door pull shut, followed by a familiar click of the lock.

My head was light, the deep colors of the room were brighter to me, and even from across the room, I could feel the fire's glow, as though I sat on the hearth.

I curled up on my side and held my burned hand out in front of me. I rode out the after-glow of my first blood exchange and tried to ignore the lonely ache deep inside me, not for David, or for home, but for the strange creature who had taken me against my will and held me captive. It was a sickness to want to know him, not just about his kind; the man who had fought his own brother to protect me. I 'd heard pain in his voice as he begged me to let him heal me. Those weren't the actions of a monster.

The darkest feeling in me was the war between everything I had known before and my fascination with the emerald-eyed stranger whose tainted blood still coated my tongue with metallic sweetness and ran through my veins like fire.

Chapter 12

There was sunlight on my face when I awoke. It was so bright against my eyelids that I was afraid to open them so I lay very still and listened for anything that could tell me where I was. Still air and the musky smell of old stone and the passage of centuries surrounded me. I gathered my bravery enough to crack one eyelid. I was in the fortress or castle, after all, but not in my room. I forced myself to unwind the bandage from my hand while I was still partially hidden by my bedding, as though it would also protect me from whatever I would find.

I drew in a shaky breath as the bandage fell away to reveal almost unblemished skin. Only the barest marking of the burn remained. It was weeks— maybe months— healed. I didn't know if that was from the vampire blood or if I had been held even longer while I was unconscious. Either way, I wasn't about to be killed and that thought gave me the bravery to poke my head out completely and look around.

So much light surrounded me I could almost convince myself that I hadn't been kidnapped at all. I had fallen, bumped my head, and woken up here and in my inured state conjured dreams that combined my history and life with the Venatores. Then I looked again and my heart sank into the pit of my stomach. The windows were high up and while sunlight had fallen on my face, I could see the gears and pulleys that would drop a metal cover over them, shutting any trace of light out.

Along the walls were bright, well-preserved tapestries. They hung all around the room and told, in the most graphic pictures, a story of violence and death: a story where vampires hunted peasants and aristocrats alike and bathed in the blood of their victims. Such grisly displays made my stomach heave. Still, I had to get off the island of comfort that I hid in and the door was only a few steps away.

I slipped out of the bed and my feet landed silently without even a whisper as my bare soles hit the stone floor. The stone itself wasn't cold to the touch and belatedly I realized I didn't feel cold at all, even though I was naked. It was as though the air had warmed itself to the temperature of my skin. Or, I thought with a shudder, my skin had cooled to the temperature of the air. I felt my wrist and was relieved to find a strong, steady pulse there.

I wrapped myself in a coverlet from the end of the bed for modesty's sake, and slunk to the door. I reached out with my ability to feel for signs of anyone on the other side of the door. I felt no presence, but received something like a sonar image of a stone corridor that turned a corner not far from the door. I inhaled sharply, pleased with how much my skill had grown and how much clearer the image was than any I'd gotten before.

Of course, the door was locked from the outside and I kicked it angrily, stubbing my toe, hard. My eyes teared up and I pressed my back to the wall, biting off a curse. I held my breath and listened. When no sound came from the other side, I released the breath I'd been holding and continued to inspect my surroundings.

I dropped the blanket and wandered around the room, touching furniture, books, anything within reach, reveling in the sensation of the different textures under my skin. I looked down at my hands. My hands and arms were still mine but like I was wearing a new skin for the very first time. I found the only truly familiar thing in the room when I sat in a high-backed chair and drew my knees up to my chest, heels resting on my bare buttocks.

I happened to glance next to my seat and all by itself, lying on the table as though it was left for me, was the leather packet that contained Dominique's spells. In the light of day, they were far easier to read, and I retied the leather thong and lifted it into my lap. Underneath it was a small piece of parchment, folded in half. I opened it and read the note.

Lady Caroline,

> *It grieves me to have to use such an impersonal method to give you such a deeply personal piece of news. However, if my business detains me, you cannot wait until night has fallen to learn what I am about to speak of.*

> *I will keep my promise of returning your own foster brother to your people. However, I cannot promise that violence will not follow back to us. You were taken with war in mind and though I know you wished to leave with him, that, I cannot allow. You will understand more as night falls, but you are likely already feeling the effects of the blood exchange between us. When the sun goes*

down, you'll feel it more, and you will need to be with us to avoid the dangers thereof.

I must thank you. In finding David, you unwittingly uncovered my brother's ambitions, which have increased these last decades while he was leading the coven. I was not aware of my brother's ability to block me from his mind and once I pulled the thread that you uncovered his plan to replace me as Master of the City was exposed. I do not know the breadth of his betrayal. For this reason, you have been moved to my own quarters, for your safety.

As intriguing to me as you are, I would not have wished for this to be the reason you stay with us and I hope that you understand no deception was intended when I healed you. I thought only of healing your injury, which was most severe.

Most Sincerely Yours,

Lord Nicholas De Elbrecht

I read the note again, then stood and examined my body. My hand, if possible, looked even more healed than it had minutes before. I shuddered, cold despite the absolute lack of a chill on my skin. If this was what vampire blood did to me in the warm light of day, how much more did I have to look forward to when night fell? Determined to rise to the challenge, I tried to clear my mind. There were no clothes in sight for me and I hoped that meant someone was coming for me. As if my thoughts were being read, I heard the metal on metal grind of the pulley system above my head and the metal covers clattered into place, sinking the room, and me, into darkness.

My eyes adjusted fast and I could tell the depths of shadow apart, so when the door opened, I could see the difference between the dark inside the room and the heavier dark of the hall outside. Nicholas entered the room and I covered myself as best I could with my limbs, watching him. When he realized I was out of bed, his face turned and I could tell from the flash from his eyes he had found me. He picked up the fallen coverlet and swung it over me, letting me tuck it in around myself.

"You will have help to dress soon," he said curtly.

"I only want Rachel to help me," I replied. He dipped his head in agreement.

"Thank you," I replied.

"You can see me."

"A little," I admitted. "You're a less dark shadow on black, but I can see you."

"Are you angry?" His voice was devoid of emotion, but there was regret in his words.

"I was in so much pain, I couldn't have told you no if I wanted to.

"As soon as the others had him, all there was, was blinding pain," he reminded me

"You felt my pain?" His form paced until, with a curse, he bent toward the fireplace and a flame leaped from the logs.

"Yes, I could feel, or, rather hear, your pain, screaming in my head." I nodded, and glanced toward the fire. "How did you do that?"

"That, well, that was just natural gas and an ignitor, you could've started it anytime you wanted." He looked away from me and cleared his throat, while I sat back, feeling like an idiot.

"So, not vampire magic?" I said drily. He turned to face me, and the air whooshed out of my chest. His face, ruggedly handsome even in its usual brooding expression, was made irresistible by his smile. I closed my mouth and tried to hide the blush that I felt climbing my spine to spread over my chest and shoulders to my face. I dropped my eyes and went still as his shadow fell over me.

When I looked up from under my eyelids, he was over me, his face as close as he had been the night before. The memory of his touch made my heart speed up and I licked my lips, trying desperately to think of something to say, that would make him stop staring into my eyes with that hunger.

"You are such an old soul, for one so tender in years," he whispered softly. My body trembled from the brush of his breath over what little skin was exposed and I wished I'd covered even more of myself with the blanket.

His lips brushed my forehead and I turned my face up to him as his lips came down again, brushing my lips once, twice, and then again with a deeper kiss, until I pricked my tongue on a fang and the swift pain brought me back to myself.

"You were in my head!" I gasped, ineffectually shoving against his chest. He stepped back from me, anger plain on his face for a split second, before it smoothed out to its usual unreadable calm.

"Whatever gives you peace from your hypocrisy, my lady," he said coolly. I knew that he hadn't done any more than I wanted him to and bit my lip to stop talking. I changed the subject before I was forced to face my own desire for not just that kiss, but more; so much more I didn't understand what it was I wanted. He spun on one heel and strode toward the door.

"Wait," I called out, my voice cracking with emotion, "Please don't go. Not like this." He turned his head toward me.

"Then how should I go?"

"Please stay with me. How long have I been here? I have been alone in the dark for years, it seems. I thought you wanted to talk to me." He slowly turned his body to face me.

"Perhaps I should find someone else to speak with me. A Venatores hunter is not an appropriate choice in a consigliore or liaison with the outside world."

I raised an eyebrow at his words.

"It would seem to me that there is no one better to advise you on the world than someone who lives on both sides of the veil between humanity and the creatures of the night" I countered, tucking my cover under my arms and pushing it in at my sides so it looked like a dress. "I still want to go home. But, you and Rachel, and even Colette, in her half-crazed way, have taken care of me and tried to keep me safe. Let me do what you had me here for."

He slowly walked back to the fire and sat in the other chair. He looked me over and I flushed again, my eyes dropping to my lap.

"Why do you do that? Drop your eyes like an errant child under the scrutiny of a parent?" he asked, a smile playing at the corners of his mouth when I glanced at him.

"You remember having parents?" I asked, amazed.

"Not as much as I have experienced being the parent, of sorts. These are monsters to you. To me, they are my children, the good ones and those who vex me, equally."

My shoulders sagged. "You aren't all monsters," I admitted. "But, Vittorio won't be punished for what he did to me and David?" I asked him, doing my best to keep my voice measured and calm.

"He is already being punished. He will not be killed so don't ask for it. He's special to me. He was my brother before we were turned and is the last surviving member of my birth family. And now, it is time for you to answer my questions, tiny hunter." His voice was gentle. He smiled at me and my heart melted.

"But you have so much more to teach me. What can I do, tell you the best cell phone provider and steer you toward the coolest clothing stores? I'm seventeen and I feel younger in terms of the world. I don't know anything, except what the Venatores want me to. Because of you, now I know that's practically nothing." I took a breath. "But you must know so much, about where I'm from, and what I can do with this ability in my head." I leaned forward and touched his hand without thinking, forgetting to breathe as electricity shot through me. I sat back and twisted my fingers together, afraid to look in his eyes.

"You are very brash, for one who seems so afraid of herself." He chuckled and my eyes met his as I glanced up in surprise.

"I'm not afraid of myself, I'm afraid of everything else," I corrected him, embarrassed and ashamed.

"And yet, the only times I've seen you afraid, have been when you were confronted with your own power, your own emotions, and your own beauty."

I crimsoned, my face hot. He leaned forward and took my hand, making me tremble as a tingling sensation pulsed through my body. "You are beautiful, and wise, it is easy to forget how young you are."

"How old were you, when you were changed?" I asked taking my hands back from his grip.

"I was twenty-two years old. Almost a man," he scoffed. "Vittorio was nineteen. Even then, he had a predilection for causing fear in women. He preferred them uncertain and unbalanced when he courted them."

I shook my head at him. "I admit, this blanket is not enough cover if he's going to be the topic." I shuddered as the mood changed with mention of his brother's name.

"We are, who we are. When we're infected, we don't change; we simply become more of who we already are. Hunting our food is necessity. Not all are cruel, some refuse human blood altogether. Others," he sighed and stared into the fire, "others were never human, and they too become even more monstrous than they were."

"But you let them live," I coaxed, and he scoffed and stood, towering over me with the flames behind him, casting an eerie shadow.

"You live among hunters, who do not discern between good or evil, but if given the chance will hunt everything and anything that is different from them and you presume to judge me?" he stated. His voice was cold and flat and my mouth dried up even as my palms dampened. "What exactly was your brother up to, when you were taken? He is a predator too, after all. How long would you have looked the other way as he used his ability to prey on the women around him?"

"He can't help it!" I began, but something in his eyes made me stop. "You have that same ability," I accused him. "I've felt it and seen it work."

"But you do not feel it now, do you?" He asked, coldly. For the second time in hours, tears stung my eyelids as I realized the truth of what he said.

"I think you were right, after all. I'm sorry I asked you to stay, you have much more important business to attend to," I said, proud that my voice, at least, did not betray the pain I felt as I thought about how long I had desired David, possibly against my own will.

"I'll send Rachel to you. You need to be dressed before you say goodbye to your David."

"He's not my—" I started to argue, but slammed my mouth shut and nodded. He left without a sound, besides the loud click of the door being locked, and I was left reeling from the understanding that my best friend had used his glamor on me for years, to manipulate me. It wasn't until I felt the darkness fall over the last rays of a sunset I couldn't even see, that I realized I had failed to ask what should have been the most important question of all. What was going to happen to me now?

Chapter 13

It was only a few minutes before Rachel joined me, her arms full of fabric. She didn't greet or speak to me and I was afraid that my last words with her master had pushed him too far. I obediently stood and moved as she gestured, helping her dress me, and tried to fight my tears. She had been kind, almost warm, but it was my fault for forgetting what she was, and what I was to her.

"I'm sorry," I whispered, the words slipping out without my meaning them to. I thought of Simi, the bold, brash hunter who had pushed me harder than any of the others in my class, and Dominique, who had told me I was special and given me her own spells to learn from on my own. I was apologizing to the vampire for being a hunter. But, in my thoughts, it was the hunter's I was too ashamed to face again.

I felt a hand on my shoulder and when I turned, the eyes peering into mine weren't angry, but sympathetic. Rachel winked at me and walked over to the wall nearest the bookshelves. She turned an old-fashioned switch I'd missed in my exploration of the room and low, flickering Edison bulbs glowed. She motioned me to her and when I got close enough, she pulled down the collar of her dress to show me a long, crooked line of dried blood across her throat. I gasped and she folded her collar up.

"Who?" I asked, but I was sure I knew. "Nicholas?" I suggested, and she shook her head. "Vittorio." I growled. She set her mouth in a thin line. "How?" I asked then waved my hands. "I'm sorry. It's not my place, even if you could speak."

"Oh, she'll be talking soon enough," said a low, husky voice that sent chills down my spine.

"Hello, Colette," I replied, staring wide-eyed at Rachel, but managing to keep my voice calm.

"Witch," the vampire whined, "I'm losing my plaything because of you."

"And here I was thinking you were alive because of me," I scoffed. Rachel gave me her arm, as though to escort me, and placed herself between us.

"The coffin wouldn't have killed me. It won't kill Vittorio either. But you had best hope that the master doesn't decide to make you his servant and keep you, because his brother will only be crazier and angrier when he finally gets out." I paused and looked her in the eyes.

"What do you mean?" I asked. Rachel prodded me ahead and I glared at her before moving.

"That's for the master to share, not me," Colette gloated. I made a rude noise at her and let Rachel escort me. I was fully aware that I was only brave with her at my side. Colette wanted me to ask, which made me want to do anything but. However, even as I silently swore to say nothing to him, my curiosity grew.

Rachel led me along the corridor and down the sweeping staircase. It curved around, just as I'd seen when I'd reached out with my ability. Emboldened by my earlier success, I tried again. I lowered my eyelids and let Rachel be my eyes while I reached out with my mental "fingers" of psychic power and looked ahead. At the bottom of the stairs, I saw two vampires, standing on either side of the staircase in servant's uniforms, with white linen shirts tucked in to black fitted trousers, with matching black vests and white gloves.

The light was brighter at the bottom of the stairs than it had been in either of the quarters I'd been held in.

It occurred to me that while the room was the Master's, he probably spent very little time there. In the large foyer at the bottom of the stairs, a chandelier hung glittering high above our heads, and more lights shone from sconces on every wall. The entrance was ahead of us and as I turned I saw a double door that mirrored the one I'd just been facing. It led under the stairs and was also manned by footmen.

I was led through the interior doors, which were served by another set of vampire footmen, and then we walked down the stairs toward the ballroom. The sheer amount of gold in the ceiling and walls was staggering, and it served to amplify the light from the giant chandeliers that hung on each end of the dance floor.

"Is there a ball tonight?" I murmured to Rachel, once I found my voice.

"No. There is an emissary from the Venatores lamiae arriving to collect your hunter-friend." Her voice was rough and raw and barely more than a whisper because of her injuries. I felt a stab of shame that I'd forgotten her injury in my panic at the scene before me.

Knowing how fast my hand had healed, I was afraid to even speculate at the severity of her original injury.

I could infer from the number of servants alone that Nicholas wanted to impress upon the visiting hunters both his civility and his strength. Fear speared through me like ice and I clung to Rachel as if I was still a child and she could protect me. But, it wasn't the vampires lounging in every corner and at every table that overlooked the ballroom floor that I was afraid of. It was the bloodshed I was becoming increasingly certain was about to occur.

"Rachel, tell me, how long have we been here?" I glanced up at her, but I couldn't stop looking into every shadow, trying to count the number of vampires behind the vast amount of power being pushed at me.

"Only a few days," Rachel said quietly, her whisper full of gravel.

"A few days," I repeated. "It feels like forever. I want to go home, but..." I sighed and turned away from her scrutiny.

She found me a bench against a wall and even though it meant there were vampires above me I couldn't see, I felt safer there, under the bright lights. I stared around me, knowing my eyes were too wide and afraid, and my blood was pounding through my veins too fast. I tried to control both as best I could. Even so, when I saw Nicholas burst through the doors, all logical thought fled my mind.

He was dressed in red and black, his tight, shiny leather pants laced up the front and tucked into boots that hit him just above the knee. His shirt was silk, a red so dark, it looked like it had been dipped in fresh blood before he put it on. It was unbuttoned low on his chest, framing the flawless white marble of his chest and throat beneath the black scruff along his jaw. Rachel tipped my face up to her and gently shut my mouth at the same time, keeping eye contact with me until I came back to myself.

"What was that?" I managed to cough out.

"Not for you," she whispered in her harsh, grated tone. I nodded and stared at her while I built up my psychic shield. "Faster, next time," she chided, and stretched her head to the left, and then the right. "Getting better," she added softly, patting the cameo in the hollow at the base of her throat.

I watched as a group of musicians descended the stairs and sat in the corner across the room from me. They tuned their instruments and began a waltz, and I watched as vampires filled the floor for a dance. The musicians had no power when I tried to reach out to them, and I realized that they were more human even than I was. There was no taste of power of any kind and I watched the vampires around them, dancing in sweeping, graceful circles across the floor.

"Not a ball, huh?" I asked, shooting Rachel a look. She smiled and shrugged. "We put on our show, then the Venatores put on their show, and then we get to business." I looked around for anyone who stood out as a hunter among the vampires, but they hadn't arrived, that I could see anyway.

Occasionally I caught a glimpse of Nicholas, leaning over the hand of some female vampire or other, or speaking closely with one of the vampires I assumed were his lieutenants. He was so handsome and untouchable. I was afraid he'd never come to me after irritating him in his quarters.

The air grew static with anticipation as vampires opened themselves up and pushed out with their power, flexing for each other and deafening me with the sheer press of psychic energy against me. I stretched my jaw and tried to pop my ears, but the pressure was steady and unyielding. My fidgeting increased as my discomfort grew, and the musicians played on without a skipped beat, completely unaware of the danger they were in.

I glanced up at Rachel and shook my head, jerking to my feet. I needed to get out of that room, away from all that power, before I imploded from the forces pressing against my skull and ribcage. She took my hand and tried to help me walk, as I leaned against the wall for ballast, but I felt one last push; something new, different from any of the posturing vampires, or Nicholas, or even Vittorio. The violent stab broke the damn in my head.

I released every ounce of power clinging to my mind, shaking it off like a wet dog and flinging to every corner of the room. My chest was heaving as I tried to fill my lungs. Vampires on the dance floor faltered and even those standing against the rails above staggered back in shock as I expelled every ounce of energy and sagged, shaking, against Rachel.

"Little fool," she hissed, and glanced around furtively, looking for an escape, as the vampires all turned and honed in on me. In an instant, Nicholas was upon me, his hands on my waist, before he spun me out onto the dance floor.

"I can't dance, I can't even feel my feet from all that power," I whispered in a panic, even though whispering was useless in a room full of super-predators with preternatural hearing.

"Then it's just as well you can't shield right now," he replied glibly. I felt him enter my mind, a gentle, sensuous touch that showed me images of my limbs moving in time with his, making me feel the way my feet should step with the beat. I stared into his jewel-green eyes and let myself fall, trusting him to keep me safe and not let me make a fool of myself. In that moment, I understood that they were the same goal.

"I'm sorry," I whispered so softly it was almost just a movement of my lips. He gave a small nod and I knew he recognized I meant for more than just losing control of my shielding.

"They know you're powerful now. I don't know if I can keep you out of our turmoil. You must go with the Venatores," he admitted. His voice and eyes seemed as unhappy with the prospect as I was about leaving him. Vampires stared from every corner as we swayed together, my body pressed to his.

"I'm sorry. I'll stay without complaining, I promise. I'll do whatever you need." I suddenly felt black despair at the thought of leaving him, so many questions unanswered; so much about him I still wanted to learn. He twirled me and held me close by turns, dancing until I felt dizzy and weak in the knees. I wanted to dance with him for the rest of the night, and long after. I felt him in my mind and tilted my head so he could kiss me again. My fingers grazed jaw and my other hand went to his chest over his heart. I felt it beating stronger than I ever thought possible, in time to mine.

I felt his fingers in the loose curls of hair at my neck, and then, nothing. He stiffened and pulled away from me. Before I could register my shock and disappointment I heard a familiar voice behind me and felt Nicholas' presence leave my mind and shut the door behind him. He had repaired my shield and protected me, without my knowing it. The invasive breadth of his power quickly brought me to myself and I turned to face the men and women standing at the top of the stairs. They were men and women for sure!

Dominique stood with them, her eyes soft and concerned as they met mine. However, Eldritch and Somayo, one of our lead hunters, looked down at me with open disgust, and Simi wouldn't meet my eyes at all. Somayo moved to one side so I could see that David had been hidden behind his massive frame. He was still pale and his cuts and bruises lay in sharp relief to the whiteness of his normally tan Latino complexion. He stepped forward and glared balefully at me out of his one good eye and I felt my chin jut in automatic response to his judgement.

"Nicholas, Master of Los Angeles, we greet you," Professor Eldritch called out, while the hunters all pointed weapons close to the vampires, if not quite *at* them. I took a deep breath and waited for Nicholas to speak. He stepped forward, putting himself between me and my people and I made a sound of dismay and argument, before a nudge of power from him stole the sound from my lips. I clutched at my throat and looked around for Rachel, who was watching the scene from a position near the human musicians, her skirt hiked up to show a long knife in a garter.

"You look well, Lady Borgia," Nicholas said, turning toward the sorceress. "The centuries have been good to you."

"You as well, my lord De Elbrecht," she replied without inflection. "Now that we have reminded everyone in the room of who is titled, and who is not, perhaps we can get on with the exchange." Nicholas gestured toward David and I tried to creep around his side to better see the hunters that were still stacked up behind Eldritch.

"You still have something of ours, *my lord*," Somayo reminded him, his voice dripping with sarcasm at the title. Nicholas' chin went up and Somayo staggered as a wall of power slammed into him, and only him.

"When you are outnumbered and outgunned, hunter, it would serve you to remember your manners," a pale-haired vampire said. He strode into the center of the dance floor to stand slightly behind me, to the left of his master. Nicholas held up a hand and the lieutenant fell silent, standing at ease, his icy eyes fixed on the large black hunter who was still recovering his land legs from the blast.

A second, female vampire came up on the other side of us, to stand just at my back. Her power prickled along my skin until I turned my head and glared at her. She eyed me with jade cat-eyes but pulled her power back until I could stand it without discomfort. I brushed her with my own, as a warning, and she closed herself off completely.

Before I could gloat over my small victory, David stepped forward, taking the arm of another hunter as he descended the first two stairs before stopping. My heart soared when I saw it was Clayton and with a gasp I jerked forward to go to him, happy tears brimming over my eyelashes. I managed two steps before a third vampire lunged between us and grabbed my arm, hard enough that I felt the bone of my wrist grind together under the pressure.

I screamed in pain and leaped back to the safety of Nicholas' arms, cradling my arm and staring helplessly at my foster brother and my friend. With a growl, Nicholas shoved me back against the female vampire and lashed out with his fist. I saw a spray of ruby liquid fly from the vampire's face as his nose was crushed. The vampire fell to the floor and some other vampires picked him up and carried him off to the side of the dance floor, their frocks and trousers getting splashed by the still free-flowing blood.

"Send her to us, Nicholas," Dominique commanded. "We do not wish to spill any more blood tonight."

"Any more than you did retrieving your hunter, you mean?" he scoffed. "He was in my care, a guest, not a prisoner. You could have waited until the exchange, but honor isn't a value known to your kind, is it?"

"Honor?" Eldritch bellowed. He limped forward and slid his sword free of its cane/sheath. Dominique reached out to stop him and he shot her a withering look that made her step back. "Don't think there's any pity for witches who consort with demons, Borgia." I quailed at his words, waiting for lightning to strike him for speaking out against her, but she pressed her lips together in a thin line and stood her ground without argument. I looked to David and Clayton for help to prevent Eldritch from starting a bloodbath, which, with the ratio of vampires to hunters, had only one possible outcome. Clayton's face was determined, but calm, and I risked a smile at him, reaching out to him with my thoughts on the remote chance he could hear me tell him how glad I was to see him.

I felt him recoil at the touch of my mind and his eyes widened in fear before he looked away and wouldn't meet my gaze again. I looked at David and he stared back with sick satisfaction at our friend's physical recoil from me. There was no stalemate and there was no agreement. The entire ballroom was filled with violent anticipation, leaving a tang of fear and dread like ozone in the air.

I glanced back at the musicians, all slack-faced and unaware. Rachel was standing guard over them, as much from the vampires, I realized, as from overzealous hunters. I felt panic rearing its ugly head inside me and gathered all my strength, waiting for a blow from one side or the other. I knew I was an enemy to both now, but did not understand why.

Nicholas pressed me against the long, hard line of his body, and my panic began to subside. I looked at David and understood his hatred. I'd been taken against my will and had been lavished, in his mind, with honor and gifts. He'd followed Colette, the lure, out of sheer stupidity and lust, and his broken bones were his reward.

"This isn't my fault, David," I said, my voice ringing out louder than I intended in the taut silence of the room. "You chose to follow the lure. You admitted to enjoying being her food. Your choices, your consequences." He snarled and leaned forward, but Clay held him back. Clayton glanced at me in confusion, and I knew without a doubt that wasn't the story David was telling.

"And what about you and your new master?" David demanded. "Whore." He spat the insult at me, but I felt nothing but disinterest in his self-pity, and disgust that he'd chosen to manipulate me, when I gladly gave him my loyalty long before he decided to use me as his practice target.

"Better the vampire with a sense of honor, than the would-be hunter who thinks mind-raping girls for fun is a worthy pastime." My voice broke and I shook with anger. At my glance, Clay automatically jerked away from David, as though he wanted to avoid any over spill of my rage.

"Enough." Nicholas didn't raise his voice, yet it rang out over the room and pressed down on the rising energy like a damper. "As you can see, you are surrounded. Since you have what you came for, I suggest you leave, before the Venatores lamiae find themselves short several hunters." I spun around and faced him.

"No," I said softly. "Back away and let them go. I will stay as your hostage, but no more threats. Please."

"Do you understand that they killed my people to collect him?"

I nodded.

"I do, and I understand that means I will be punished for them," I glanced back at my friends current and former, and mentors. "These people are *my* family. I would do anything to keep them safe, just like you would for yours." My whole body shook with fear and my stomach heaved, but I stood firm. "I accept the punishment for the murders these hunters committed. They were just trying to save us. We were foolish, and ignorant of the world, despite what we know."

Domonique's eyes widened, but she said nothing. David scoffed, and turned away. Professor Eldritch was the one who spoke up first.

"Do you have any idea what you've done, girl?" he muttered. He grabbed David by the shoulder and pushed him back toward the stairs.

"She's his whore. He won't hurt her."

I didn't bother to refute his evil words. I had fed from the master and he from me. The hunters wouldn't care if it was to save me.

"I am no one's whore, David. But, I am especially not yours." I raised my voice so that the hunters on the stairs could hear me clearly. "I hope someone teaches my foster brother to control his mind-rape ability, before he crosses the wrong person and brings dishonor on you all." I shrugged at the professor.

"You will die," he said, softer, staring into my eyes as if to make me understand. He wasn't angry. If anything, I noted, he was proud of me.

"But, I will die with honor," I replied. I gathered the power that had attracted the attention of all the vampires— that hidden store that I felt deep inside me— and focused. "You should go, quickly." My plan was to simply blast out all the energy I had in me and hope it cut down on the vampires they had to fight on the way out.

Instead, I saw a flash of light from the top of the staircase as Lady Borgia set off a flash grenade. Blinded, I dropped to my knees automatically, my body kicking into training mode from all the work and obstacle courses Simi had put me through. I felt a tap on my shoulder and shifted to the left, staying low. Vampires and hunters clashed at the base of the stairs and my voluminous skirts got in the way as I tried to help the hunters fight their way back toward the door.

I felt a hand on my shoulder and Professor Eldritch was there, Nicholas at his back. I tried to warn him, but Nicholas grabbed us both and suddenly I was at the top of the stairs with the professor standing next to me. Nicholas was ahead of us, in the doorway, and motioned for us to follow him. I looked back, trying to find David, or Clay, or Simi, but they were too far to call to without attracting the attention of every vampire between us. Eldritch grabbed my good arm and shoved me ahead of him, and I shook my head.

"I can fight!" I hissed.

"I know you can. But, you have a power that needs to be protected. Go with him now. We'll come find you. I promise," he bellowed over the din of the fight. I finally obeyed, looking back only once to see my professor fighting a vampire with his sword.

Nicholas ducked to one side as more vampires and hunters battled in the grand foyer and led me through a labyrinthine set of corridors that took us deep underground. Together we ran faster and faster until I skidded to a stop, amazement on my face. He laughed and took my hand, turning another corner and stopping outside a forbidding steel door.

"Through this room, is your freedom. It is a back door of sorts." He opened the door to a room lit only by torches hung on the walls to each side. There were doors at the far end and a single coffin in the middle, wrapped in heavy chains.

I walked closer to it and it began to shake. Ragged screams echoed from inside, making me jump back in alarm. I pulled Nicholas back into the hall we'd just come through.

"Vittorio?" I stammered, clutching Nicholas' hand. He nodded and tugged me past it, to a door on the other side. Through it, was a short hall with a door at the other end.

"There is a path that will take you to the top of the hill."

I shook out the heavy skirts. "Will I be able to run without you by my side, or should I leave this here?" I asked.

"It will fade, but for a few days, you are almost as fast as a vampire." It explained why vampires seldom kept human servants, if the blood exchange gave the human so much more than it did the vampire.

"Wait," I asked, grabbing Nicholas' hand and holding him tight as he turned to go back into the room with the horrifying vampire prison. "What are you going to do?" He ran his fingers over my cheek and slid his hand behind my head, fisting my hair as he pulled me to him.

"I'm going to get your hunters out of there. Go home, sweet, young Caroline. I will always find you and you will always know when I'm near."

"I will know you, because of my power, just as I will know when Vittorio is freed from his cage," I argued, selfishly stalling, even though my friends were fighting for their lives.

"Your psychic gift is now strong and will be stronger once you come back to me." He kissed me then and the heat in my body leapt to a fever pitch as his fangs gently scraped over my tongue and lips. He managed not to pierce me. I was finally leaving, but all I wanted was more of that kiss.

"There's a trick to kissing a vampire," I whispered, stroking my finger over the cool skin of his hand before backing away.

"There are many things I look forward to teaching you, Caroline," he said, his voice full of dark promises.

"Take care, tiny hunter, that you come back to me in one piece." I trembled and he ran his fingers down the low neckline of my dress, making my legs rubber. "Now, run Caroline, go."

I walked through the little wooden door and when it closed behind me, I couldn't see anything suggesting an underground fortress lay behind it. I tried the latch and it was locked tight. It stung my hand with the energy from the spells that kept people from wandering in unannounced.

I left the underskirts next to the door in case Rachel ever came looking for them. I picked up the skirts of the rest of the dress and held it around my waist as I ran. The trees and bushes flew by me in the light reflected by the moon and I ran full out, my good arm holding my skirts, my injured one pressed against my chest. Even as I ran, I felt the pain lessening in my arm and soon I could hold it by my side with a fraction of the pain it had been in before.

The vampire blood would fade, Nicholas had said, but as I wiggled the fingers on my right hand, I was grateful for it. He had sacrificed power to heal me and the thought warmed and thrilled me. I slowed my run and tried to sense vampires or hunters, but there was no one immediately near me.

I kept moving until Dominique reached out to me and when I sensed her presence, I slowed my run, trying to see everything around me. I then slowed more to a walk as I reached a paved road. I walked along the edge, drawing closer to Dominique's power, until I saw a car ahead of me, pulled over to the side. A door opened and in the light from the overhead dome, I saw Clay inside. I staggered towards it, suddenly overcome with emotion, and the realization that I was truly free and going home.

Clayton splinted my arm and made a sling out of fabric from my skirt, even though I explained that I was much better. I saw regret in his eyes and knew he was trying to make up for what had happened between us in the ballroom. Simi— that beautiful, brilliant woman I was afraid I'd never see again— wrapped me in a blanket and held me in her muscular arms all the way to the safe house in Burbank, California. I didn't complain.

It was Clay who got me alone as I stepped out of the shower, dressed and towel-drying my hair. He called me over to him in a corner and handed me a tumbler of whiskey, which I took after checking to see if any of the adults were going to stop me.

"What happened back there?" I finally asked. I hadn't spoken the whole ride, too afraid that I would find out that everyone else had died. But when I saw Eru Somayo guarding the door, and another hunter I didn't recognize nodding us through to the suite I was sharing with Dominique and Simi, sheer relief almost made me cry.

"Nicholas showed us all why he is the master of the city," he replied. "Both sides had injuries but no one on our side died. It was like being caught in a whirlwind. I never want to go through that again."

"And David?"

"Eldritch thought it best to send him somewhere else, with the other hunters. You're too special to risk and he's too angry to trust." He paused, and touched my shoulder gently. "Are you going to be all right?" he asked, as I sniffed, then gingerly sipped the amber liquid that burned its way from my mouth to my stomach. I shrugged and nodded, then handed him back the glass. I jerked my thumb toward my bunk.

As I lay there, I heard them talking in low whispers about my mental health and psychic ability, and how much counseling I would need to recover from my ordeal. I stretched both arms above my head and smiled to myself, relishing my "vampire" abilities while I still had them. Soon, I would go back to being just Caroline, dorky kid in school who tripped over her own feet and was everyone's first choice for "whose paper to cheat off".

But now I had something no one else had, or could take away from me. I ran my fingers over my lips and called up the memory of his mouth on mine: the sweet, metallic tang of blood under the mints he devoured to appear less monstrous. I felt him in my head and knew he was close, watching over me, keeping me safe.

"You will come back to me, tiny hunter," he reminded me and I watched a shadow pass over my window. I sighed, trying not to cry over the things I was sure I would now never learn. I rolled over and bunched up the pillow in my arms and with a start realized there was something under the pillow.

I slid the familiar leather-bound sheaf of parchment out and glanced out the window. Nicholas *was* close, even if I couldn't see him. He would never be too far away and once his kingdom was back in order, and I was old enough to choose where I would go, I would see him again.

The End

Subscribe to our Newsletter!

This exclusive **VIP Mailing List** will keep you updated on our latest content. Subscribe and receive "The Vampire Kiss" absolutely FREE to your email and stay in touch with the latest updates to your email by clicking below.

GET ACCESS NOW

www.PersiaPublishing.com/subscribe-to-romance/

LIKE US AT

https://www.facebook.com/LucyLyonsRomance/

CAN YOU HELP?!

PLEASE leave a quick review for this book if it gives you any value. It provides valuable feedback that allows me to continuously improve my books and motivates me to keep writing.

Thank You!

19499244R00102

Printed in Poland
by Amazon Fulfillment
Poland Sp. z o.o., Wrocław